KEY DEATH

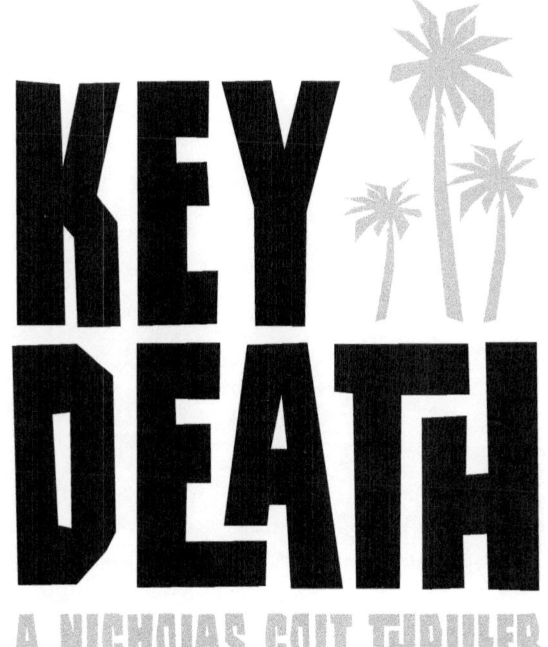

JUDE HARDIN

The characters and events portrayed in this book are fictitious. Any similarity to real persons, living or dead, is coincidental and not intended by the author.

Printed in the United States of America.

Published by Thomas & Mercer

P.O. Box 400818

Las Vegas, NV 89140

ISBN-13: 9781611098150

ISBN-10: 1611098157

Library of Congress Control Number: 2012917233

To Sue, who loves zombies.

A NOTE FROM THE AUTHOR:

Key Death grew from a short story of mine titled "Stalker," published briefly in the spring of 2012 under a pen name. The story is no longer available, and I mention this only in case anyone who might have read it finds some of the character names and situations here familiar. *Key Death* is a brand-new adventure and, unlike the previous story, told from the inimitable perspective of private investigator Nicholas Colt.

CHAPTER ONE

When I was twelve, a movie called *Time Traveling Zombie Bikers from Darkest Hell* came to the drive-in theater in Hallows Cove, Florida, where I lived with my stepfather. Supposedly it was the first in a series of low-budget horror films featuring the zombie bikers, and rumor had it *Time Traveling Zombie Bikers from Darkest Hell Visit Nazi Germany* would be coming out later in the summer.

My best friend Joe Crawford and I begged his parents to take us, and one Saturday night they finally caved. They loaded some lawn chairs and a cooler full of soft drinks and an industrial-sized bag of cheese puffs into the back of their station wagon, and off we went. The film was rated R, so it was kind of a big deal. Joe and I hoped to hear a lot of cussing and see a lot of gore, and maybe even get a glimpse of a naked breast or two.

Thirty-some years later, news of another murder down in Key West triggered the memory of that movie.

The reporter on the car radio said it was the eleventh case in a bizarre series of homicides where the killer surgically removed the victims' brains and then reattached the tops of their heads with Krazy Glue. In every case, asphyxiation was the official cause of death, but there were conflicting opinions about whether the victims were smothered before or after the initial cuts with the bone saw. My money was on after. Anyone sick enough to steal your brain is probably going to make you suffer for a while beforehand.

For obvious reasons, the mainstream media had dubbed the perpetrator of these heinous crimes The Zombie. One popular anchorperson on CNN even speculated that the killer might actually be eating the missing organs, although there was no real evidence to that effect.

Not all of the slayings had occurred in Key West, but the most recent three had, and some people—most notably a couple of smart-ass morning DJs in Jacksonville—had started calling the southernmost tip of our country *Key Death*. Tourism was down, as was the price of real estate.

"Aren't you glad we don't live in Key West?" Juliet asked.

Juliet was my date for the evening, and she also happened to be my wife. We were on our way to see John Fogerty in concert at the St. Augustine Amphitheatre.

"Some of the murders occurred up in Georgia," I said. "And some of them in other states along the coast. You never know. He might even show up in a nice little subdivision thirty miles southwest of Jacksonville. Nobody is safe from *The Zombie*."

I said it melodramatically as hell, mimicking a measure of ominous music at the end. Joking around was my way of coping with something that scared the living crap out of me.

Not serial killers.

Zombies.

Time Traveling Zombie Bikers from Darkest Hell did a number on me when I was twelve. There weren't any naked women, but the graphic violence was over the top.

Zombies have seriously freaked me out ever since.

"It's not funny," Juliet said. "I feel sorry for the families of those people. The latest victim was only twenty-eight."

"I wonder if young brains taste better than old brains. I'll have to Google that when we get home."

She slapped me on the arm. "How would you like it if you found me or Brittney with an empty skull?"

I decided not to go for the obvious joke on that one. Anyway, it would have been grossly inaccurate. Both my girls were extremely intelligent. Juliet was a registered nurse, working on her master's degree, and Brittney, our adopted daughter, was a sophomore at the University of Florida, majoring in English with the intent to apply to law school. If anyone was missing a brain, it was me, Nicholas Colt. World-class guitar player with a crippled hand, ace detective with a revoked license. I like to blame my brainlessness on too many bottles of Kentucky whiskey over the years, but the truth is I was never that smart to begin with.

I turned left into the amphitheater parking area. "Maybe The Zombie won't make it to the show tonight," I said.

"Just shut up," Juliet said, pretending to be annoyed with me.

I'd never met John Fogerty, not even back in the eighties when I played some of the world's biggest stages with my band, Colt .45. He wasn't touring much back then, and our paths just never seemed to cross.

But tonight that was going to change.

A friend of mine named Lonnie Williams played bass for the warm-up band, and he had sent me a couple of VIP passes for after the show. I was finally going to meet one of my all-time rock heroes, a man who had penned more classics than I had fingers to count them on.

I parked the car and we walked to the gate and gave the man our tickets. On the way to our seats we passed the concession stand, and I asked Juliet if she wanted anything.

"A beer, I guess. And some nachos."

I paid for the beer and the nachos, and a double bourbon on the rocks for myself.

It was going to be a great night. I could just feel it.

I had no idea it was going to set the wheels in motion for the most horrendous seven days of my life.

CHAPTER TWO

They roll up to the diner in a cloud of fog and dust and exhaust fumes. These aren't your ordinary zombies. They can talk, and even though they shuffle along in a dazed state when on foot, they somehow possess the coordination to handle motorcycles as well as any other gang of leather-clad thugs.

Their leader is a skinny guy named Rex. He has a shaved head and a goatee and eyes that ooze with bright-red blood every time he blinks. He climbs off his bike and shambles toward the diner's entrance, followed by half a dozen of his evil zombie disciples.

Not only can these zombies talk and ride motorcycles, they somehow possess the ability to travel back in time. The choppers are modern, and the boys wear bell-bottoms and tie-dyed T-shirts and peace-sign necklaces, but the diner they walk into is straight from the 1940s. Gleaming steel and chrome, nineteen-cent hot dogs, Dizzy Gillespie's "A Night in Tunisia" playing on the Seeburg jukebox in the corner.

"Brains and eggs," Rex says to the guy behind the counter. "And some coffee."

All the other walking corpses grunt and nod in agreement. They all want the same thing for breakfast. Brains and eggs.

The guy behind the counter flips the burger he has going on the grill, flicks his long cigar ash on the floor, looks at Rex and grins. "We got eggs," he says. "But we seem to be fresh out of brains today."

"Then I guess we'll have to harvest some," Rex says.

He jumps over the counter, grabs a meat cleaver and splits the cook's head open like a cantaloupe...

Fogerty rocked the place.

The house lights came up after the second encore. While four thousand people clamored toward the exits, I took Juliet by the hand and led her in the opposite direction. We'd had good seats, fourth row in the pit, so we didn't have far to go.

A guy wearing black pants and a black polo guarded the aisle leading backstage.

"Wrong way," he said.

"We're with the band," I said.

It was a joke. When I was in junior high school, it was what you said to the ticket-taker at a show or a dance to try to get out of paying admission. The guy in the black polo just crossed his arms and looked at me. He never cracked a smile.

"That shit never worked back in the day, either," I said. I flashed my VIP badge, and he waved us through.

The first thing I noticed backstage was a rack on wheels with about twenty electric guitars hanging from it. Fogerty's guitars. All makes and models, all top-of-the-line. I couldn't believe he traveled with so many. I imagined he had to employ at least two techs to keep them all strung and in tune.

My friend Lonnie was standing beside the rack, and a young woman was standing beside him. Lonnie motioned for me to come that way.

Fellow musicians are like family. If you're part of the tribe, odds are you're not going to shake a guy's hand after not seeing him for a long time.

I gave Lonnie a hug. "Good set," I said.

"Thanks, man." He turned to the young woman standing beside him. "Wanda Taylor, meet the great Nicholas Colt."

I introduced Juliet to Lonnie and his girlfriend.

"We're just going to head back and talk to John real quick," I said, motioning toward the backstage lounge area. From my position I could see Fogerty through the glass door, standing there in his trademark flannel and denim, signing the back of a woman's T-shirt with a Sharpie.

"Wanda wants to talk to you for a minute," Lonnie said.

"Sure," I said. "But I'd really like to—"

"It'll just take a minute," Wanda said. "I promise."

I looked at Juliet. "You go ahead," I said. "I'll be right there."

Juliet gave me a kiss and then headed toward the lounge. Lonnie said he was going to grab us all a beer, leaving me alone with Wanda by the rack of guitars.

She was about five-four with long blond hair and blue eyes. She wore fashionably tattered jeans and a tank top that showed off her breasts. Suede jacket, leather stewardess bag. A little pale and a little thin. She'd recently smoked some marijuana. I could smell it.

I figured she wanted to talk to me about my music. I figured wrong.

"I understand you're a private investigator," she said.

"Not anymore."

"Really? Lonnie told me—"

"I lost my license," I said. "But I still do things for people sometimes, and sometimes they offer me monetary compensation."

"So you're totally illegal, working for cash under the table."

"If that's the way you want to put it."

"OK. Well, I don't really give a shit if you have a license or not."

I looked toward the glass door. Fogerty was out of sight now. "What can I help you with?" I asked.

"I was adopted at birth, and I would like to find my biological father. I've seen the adoption records, and I've actually talked to my mother, but it seems dear old Dad is nowhere to be found."

"So you know his name?"

"I do. It's Phineas T. Carter. My mother couldn't remember what the *T* stood for, but she was pretty sure that was his middle initial."

"I take it they were never married."

"Oh, hell no," she said. "I was totally a product of a roll in the hay. Or a romp in the backseat of a car, most likely."

"How old are you?" I asked.

"Twenty-four."

Half Lonnie's age, I thought. Scoundrel.

"Why the sudden interest in finding your father?" I asked.

"I just want to know where I came from. I'd like to meet him, if he wants to. Just hang out and talk for a while or whatever. When Lonnie told me about this private-detective friend of his who was coming to the show tonight, it sounded like a good opportunity to get the ball rolling."

"What else did Lonnie tell you about me?"

"I know you had a southern rock and blues band in the eighties called Colt Forty-Five. I know you were the sole survivor of a plane crash that killed your wife and baby daughter and everyone in your band. I know you can't use your left hand to play guitar anymore because a guy in Tennessee—"

"Lonnie told you all that?"

"He didn't have to. Most of it's on your Wikipedia page. Plus, I'm a pretty good rock historian all by myself, Mr. Colt. What they say about blondes isn't always true. We're not all stupid."

"You seem pretty clever to me," I said. "Probably clever enough to find your own father, if that's what you want."

"So you don't want the job?"

"I didn't say that. It's just—"

"I know what you're thinking," she said. "Another freebie. Another favor for a friend. But that's not what I want. I made it clear to Lonnie that I would pay you very well for your time. I have money, Mr. Colt. What I don't have is a true sense of my biological heritage. There's an entire half of me that I know nothing about. So here's the deal. I'll give you five thousand dollars to find my father. All you have to do is find him and give me a number where I can reach him. Is five thousand enough?"

Lonnie was standing by the glass door talking to Juliet now. He was holding two bottles of Heineken in each hand.

"Five thousand is way too much," I said. "I'll charge you what I charge everyone else. A hundred an hour. It shouldn't take more than half a day."

She opened her shoulder bag and pulled out a wad of bills. She counted out a thousand dollars. She handed me the money, along with a business card.

"Just let me know if it's going to be more than that," she said. "John Fogerty's on Letterman tomorrow night, and we're heading up to New York for a couple of more gigs with him, but I'll wire you the money from wherever I am."

"Thank you," I said. "I'll need to get some more information from you, but right now—"

Lonnie and Juliet walked our way. Juliet was making a *what's up* gesture with her hands. When they got to the guitar rack, Juliet said, "Nicholas, what are you doing? You missed him."

"What?"

"He's gone. He had an important meeting at the hotel. Said he'll catch you next time."

"He's gone?"

"Yeah. But look. I got him to sign my CD."

Well, hell.

CHAPTER THREE

The next morning it took me three and a half hours of phone calls and Internet searches to find Phineas T. Carter, who was dead. His address history put him in the right place and time to have met Wanda's mother, and a four-year stint in the navy accounted for his abrupt disappearance two months before Wanda was born. I even found a photograph from a Facebook account nobody had bothered to delete. His obit had been published in a newspaper called the *Citizen*.

Juliet was working a twelve-hour shift at the hospital, and I had the house to myself. I poured a cup of coffee, sat at the kitchen table, called Wanda Taylor and told her the bad news.

"Are you sure it's him?" she asked.

"Ninety-nine percent sure. I'm going to e-mail you a picture, and you can forward it to your mother. She should be able to tell you for sure if it's him or not."

"She knew him twenty-four years ago. I'm sure he's changed since then."

"He has a lot of ink," I said. "Full sleeve tats on both arms. I'm betting some of them are older than you are."

She paused. "My mother didn't say anything about tattoos, but I'll ask her. Where was he living? How did he die?"

"He had an apartment down in Key West. I hate to be the one to tell you this, Wanda, but your father was murdered."

"Murdered. Oh my god. In Key West? Was it—"

"I don't think it was The Zombie," I said. "Your father was shot to death in his apartment. Totally different MO."

She cleared her throat. "No, I was going to ask if it was a drug deal that went bad or something. My mother told me he used to do some smuggling. So tell me, do they know who killed my father?"

"There was an investigation, of course, but from what I've seen there was never an arrest. Or really even any credible leads. But now that you tell me he was into smuggling, it's a fairly safe bet the murder was drug-related."

"I want to know who killed my father," Wanda said. "And I want to know about him. About his life. About what kind of man he was."

I took a sip of coffee. It was lukewarm and bitter. I got up and added half a shot of Old Fitzgerald from my jug in the pantry. I sat back down at the table.

"Are you there?" Wanda asked.

"I'm here."

"I want to know who killed my father," she repeated.

"That could be tough. Maybe even impossible. If it was a drug deal—"

"I want to know, and I'm willing to pay you whatever it takes to find out."

"Me?"

"Sure. Why not?"

"You want me to go down to Key West and investigate your father's murder?"

"Yes."

I took a drink of my spiked coffee. Key West was an eight-hour drive from the nice little three-bedroom house Juliet and I bought soon after we got married. A murder investigation could take months, and I didn't want to be separated from my wife for that long. Things had been good between us for a while, and I didn't want to rock the boat.

Then again, we had a mortgage and a car payment and a kid in college, and it had been weeks since I'd made any money. The job Wanda Taylor was offering down in the Keys would be a good opportunity for me to contribute to our finances.

"I'll have to think about it," I said.

"When will you know?"

"I'll call you tonight. Just out of curiosity, why is it so important for you to find out who killed your father?"

There was a long pause, and then she said, "I'm dying, Mr. Colt. The doctors tell me I only have a few more weeks to live. Finding my biological parents was something I felt I had to do. Part of my bucket list, you know? And now that I know my father was murdered, I want to see that justice is served. Whoever was responsible for me not getting to meet my dad needs to pay."

"I'm sorry," I said. "I had no idea."

"So you'll call me tonight?"

"Yes," I said. "I'll call you tonight."

CHAPTER FOUR

The cook falls to the floor. His legs twitch a few times, and then he lies still. Rex pries his skull open, reaches in, and scoops out the delicate brain tissue. It is pink and slimy and Rex slings it on the grill and it steams and sizzles and all the other zombies grunt in approval.

"Brains!" Rex says.

"Brains!" the other zombies repeat.

"We need more brains!" Rex says.

"More brains! More brains!"

The door to the diner opens, and in walks a fat man wearing khakis and mirrored sunglasses and a silver star.

"Hey, Charlie," the fat sheriff says. He takes his sunglasses off. "Wait a minute. You're not Charlie."

"I'm Rex," Rex says. "Charlie don't work here anymore."

"Now wait just a goddamn minute. Where's Charlie?"

"Like I said, Charlie don't work here anymore."

Rex turns and flips the cook's brain with a spatula. The other zombies are sitting on stools at the counter, looking toward the obese lawman.

The sheriff rests his hand on the butt of his service revolver. "You boys own those bikes out there?"

The zombies grunt, nod.

"We ain't got no use for no motorcycle gangs around here," the sheriff says.

The zombies nod. They rise from their stools, as though they are going to comply with the sheriff's request to leave town. But you just know they aren't. You just know they are going to surround the fat redneck sheriff and rip him to pieces, and of course that's exactly what they do.

Juliet got home from work a little after eight. I was sitting on the back deck nursing a bottle of Samuel Adams Boston Lager, watching the temperature gauge on the gas barbecue creep toward the red zone.

Juliet stuck her head through the door and said, "Hey."

"Hey," I said. "Grab a beer and come on out."

"I think I better grab a quick shower first."

"OK. See you in a few."

I watched her walk away through the glass. I'd married a beautiful woman. Even in hospital scrubs, she was a beautiful woman. Something stirred inside me every time I looked at her. Half American, half Filipino. Five-three, long black hair, olive complexion. She had a movie-star smile, and eyes like an autumn afternoon. It almost made me feel guilty sometimes, how lucky I was to have her.

I drained the last of my Sam Adams. I'd started to get up and go for another when my cell phone trilled. It was Brittney.

"Hey, Daddy," she said.

"Hey. I thought you were going to that thing tonight."

A few days ago Brittney had told me the author Carl Hiaasen was going to be in Gainesville for a reading and book signing at one of the auditoriums on campus.

"I'm here," she said. "He just hasn't shown up yet. What are you doing?"

"Fixing to burn some meat," I said. "Listen, I wanted to let you know I'm going to be leaving town for a while."

"Where are you going?"

"Down to the Keys. Maybe for a few weeks."

"The Keys? I want to go!"

"You have school," I said. "Plus, I'm going on business. I'm going by myself."

"Mom's not going with you?"

"No. I haven't even told her yet."

Brittney sighed. "You know what happened that one time you went out of town on business. You almost got yourself killed. You came back with a crippled hand and addicted to heroin. And then there was that horror show up in the Okefenokee. Let's not forget about that. So what kind of business—"

"A woman hired me to find her father," I said. "She was adopted at birth, and she has a terminal illness, and she wants to meet her biological parents before she dies."

"Oh," Brittney said.

I spared her the detail that the woman's father had been murdered, probably by drug dealers. I didn't want to worry her. She had been through a lot before Juliet and I adopted her. She had been living with her sister, and had run away from home. That's where I came into the picture. Her sister hired me to find her. Brittney was with a pimp when I tracked her down, and from there it only got worse. I ended up saving her life, and then she ended up saving mine. She still suffered from recurrent nightmares about our ordeal with a religious cult called Chain of Light. She was making progress in her counseling sessions, but I frequently had to remind myself that she was still somewhat fragile emotionally.

"So what time is Carl Hiaasen supposed to be there?" I asked.

"Eight-thirty. Any minute. What about that serial killer down in Key West, Dad? Have you heard about that? Oh my god, that is so freaky."

"I've heard about it," I said. "But don't worry, I'll try to steer clear of any serial killers. Anyway, The Zombie is only interested in people with brains."

She laughed. "You're so goofy. Well, some guy on the stage just told everyone to turn their cell phones off, so I guess I better go."

"Talk to you soon, sweetheart. Love you."

"Love you too, Daddy. Bye."

I got up and walked inside and pulled another longneck out of the refrigerator. I lowered two thick slabs of raw beef onto a plate, grabbed a set of tongs, and went back outside. I set the plate and the tongs on the little table I keep by the grill. A few minutes later, Juliet joined me.

"Are you going to cook that meat, or just look at it?" she said.

"Just look at it for now. Isn't it pretty?"

"I thought I heard you talking to someone."

"It was Brittney. She was at Carl Hiaasen's book signing and they told everyone to turn their phones off, so she had to go. I was telling her about the job I'm going on."

"Job?"

I told Juliet the whole story, including the part about Phineas T. Carter being a drug smuggler.

"You're not going down there," she said. "No way. It sounds too dangerous."

"I'll be careful," I said.

"No amount of money is worth risking your life for, Nicholas. I want you here with me. I want to be with you for many more years to come."

"I will be here with you for many more years to come. But I've just been feeling so useless lately. I sit around here and drink beer and watch TV and eat pork rinds. Did you know I've gained ten pounds in the last six months? I feel like a bum. A big fat bum. I can't play the guitar anymore because of my hand, and I can't get much work as a PI because of my license. What am I supposed to do? I've been offered the opportunity to make a big chunk of change, Jules. How can I say no?"

"I make enough. You don't have to work."

She looked at me, and I could tell by the expression on her face that she knew she'd said the wrong thing. She knew there was more to it than the money. Everyone needs a sense of purpose. Without that, you might as well shrivel up and die.

"I do have to work," I said. I left it at that.

"All right, then. If you're going, then I'm going with you."

"Sure," I said. "You can just quit your job. That'll make a lot of sense."

"I won't have to quit. I have a lot of personal leave time built up. And honestly, I could use a vacation."

"I don't know."

"I do know. So it's settled. I'm going."

"What about The Zombie?" I asked.

She took a sip of her beer. "I am not scared of The Zombie. I eat zombies for breakfast."

I laughed, leaned over, and kissed her on the lips. "It's not really going to be a fun trip. I'll have to spend most of my time working."

"That's OK. At least we'll be together part of the time. And I'll be able to make sure you don't get into any trouble."

"You're something else," I said. "Will you marry me?"

She got up and used the tongs to lower the steaks onto the grill. "I'll think about it," she said. "I'll think about it."

And then I thought about it. I couldn't let her come with me to Key West. There was no way.

"Look, I really do appreciate the gesture, Jules, and I would love to have you with me, but the truth is I might be dealing with some pretty unsavory characters down there. As much as I would relish your company, I'm just not going to lead you into harm's way like that."

She sat down beside me. The air was thick with smoky meat and disappointment.

"And I was starting to get excited thinking about a vacation," she said.

"I'll take you on vacation when I get back," I said. "Anywhere you want to go."

"Really? Anywhere? You promise?"

"I promise," I said.

She kissed me, and then kissed me some more, and before we knew it the steaks had burned to ashes.

CHAPTER FIVE

Wanda Taylor showed her mother the photograph I sent of Phineas Carter, and her mother confirmed that he was the right guy. Her mother remembered some of the tattoos. Wanda gave me ten thousand dollars to get started, and she agreed on a hundred an hour plus expenses for the duration. I felt like I'd won the lottery. I didn't know where Wanda's wealth came from, and I didn't ask. She was still tagging along with Lonnie on the Fogerty tour, having fun up in New York. She said they had some dates lined up in Europe after that. I wondered how long it would be before she became too sick to carry on. Maybe she didn't even plan on doing the hospital thing. Maybe she planned on having as good a time as possible and just riding it out till the end. I didn't ask about that, either.

At some point during our discussion, it occurred to Wanda that I might be tempted to sit on the beach and drink margaritas and collect hundreds of dollars a day until she died. Not that she didn't trust me, she said. I understood her concern. As in any profession, there are unscrupulous private investigators out there, some who would screw their own mothers out of their own inheritances. I told Wanda I would take the ten grand up front, and not a penny more until I had logged at least a hundred hours—about two weeks' worth of work—and had faxed her the detailed reports on all those hours. If I found out who killed her father sooner than that, I would refund the difference. Ditto if we agreed it was futile to keep searching. If she passed away before any of that happened, which was one of her biggest concerns, the remainder of the money would go to her estate or to the charity of her choice.

Which put me on a deadline, so to speak.

I loaded my 1996 GMC Jimmy and headed to Key West on a Sunday. On the way to the interstate, I stopped by my camper on Lake Barkley to pick up a .38-caliber revolver I call Little Bill. I've had it for a long time. It's the one I like to carry when I'm working. Juliet doesn't like guns in the house, so I keep most of my firearms locked in the Airstream. All but one. There's a .357 Magnum strapped to the bottom of our bed frame, and years ago I had made sure Juliet knew how to use it. It had saved me one time from a man named Derek Wahl, who had tried to stab me with a butcher knife.

It was early November, and hurricane season was winding down, so I wasn't too worried about the weather. I'd booked a room at a hotel in town, a place I'd stayed before. I went ahead and reserved it for a week. I figured I would be there at least that long. I made sure they put me on the second floor, facing the parking lot. The rooms facing the pool made me feel boxed in, and I liked being able to look out the window and watch the traffic go by.

By the time I got there and got everything settled, it was going on seven o'clock. I walked down to the lounge, bellied up to the bar, ordered an Old Fitz on the rocks. The bartender brought it and I swirled the ice with a swizzle stick and took a long satisfying pull.

There was a guy sitting on a stool on the little stage in the corner, singing and playing acoustic guitar. His name was Wesley West. I'd seen it on the sign by the hallway leading to the lounge. He was wearing dark glasses and a beret. He wasn't very good. I probably could have outplayed him on the guitar, even with my gimpy hand. I walked over and stuffed a ten in his tip jar anyway. I knew how hard it was to make a living as a musician.

I ordered another drink and took it to a table and opened up my netbook. I Googled the address where Phineas T. Carter had been murdered, and found the real-estate company that had handled the rental agreement. Red Parrot Realty. The agent's name was Darcy Clermont.

I called her, got voice mail, and left a message. Ten minutes later, she called me back. I knew she would. Real-estate agents always do. Most of them have to hustle 24/7 to scratch out a living. They always call you back.

"My name is Nicholas Colt," I said. "I'm interested in a rental property you were handling awhile back."

I told her the address.

"That's actually a condominium," she said. "The owner had been subleasing it, but she's living there herself now. That one's not available, but I have plenty of places I could show you. Places even nicer than that one for about the same price."

"I was wondering if I could get some information from you about the former tenant," I said. "Phineas T. Carter."

"That was his name, but of course any information I have about him would be confidential."

"Was he living there with someone?" I asked.

"I really can't—"

"I know he was murdered, and I know it happened at that address. I just need to find out if he had a roommate. A girlfriend or a boyfriend or just a friend who was staying with him. I'm not going to try to sell them anything. I just want to talk."

"Are you a cop?" Darcy Clermont asked. "I've already talked to about a hundred of them."

"Private," I said. "Mr. Carter's daughter hired me to investigate his murder. She has a terminal illness, so I'm hoping to get the information she wants before...you know."

When you tell someone your client's dying, it makes them feel bad. Sometimes it makes them feel bad enough to give you the information you want. It puts them on the spot. After all, what kind of human being would withhold a harmless little piece of information from a woman on her deathbed? I've been known to tell people my clients are dying when they're really not. Technically, it's not even a lie. We're all on the way out, one way or another. It's only a matter of time.

Darcy Clermont was silent for a few beats, and then said, "Well, I really shouldn't be telling you this, but I've already told the police and they've already cleared her as a suspect, so I don't see what harm it could do. Mr. Carter was indeed living there with someone. A woman."

"What's her name?" I asked.

"Hold on. Let me see if I can pull the lease up."

I waited. The cocktail waitress asked me if I wanted another drink, and I did. She brought it. I took a sip. The guy onstage was trying to sing Jimmy Buffett's "Lovely Cruise." He was butchering it.

Darcy Clermont came back on. "Here it is. She actually cosigned the rental agreement. Her name is Pamela Wade."

"Do you have a forwarding address for her?" I asked. "Or a phone number?"

"I'm sorry, I don't. But that's her name. I remember she was very nice."

"What about the woman who owns the condominium?" I asked.

"What about her?"

"Can you give me her name and number?"

She hesitated. "Well, I guess it's no big secret, since you already know the address."

She gave me the name and number.

"Thanks so much for your time," I said. "If I'm ever in the market for some property down here, I will certainly give you a call."

I finished my drink and paid my tab, walked back up to my room, and ordered a pizza.

There was nobody by the name of Pamela Wade in the Key West white pages, but there was one in Fort Lauderdale. I ran her name and phone number through one of the online databases I use, saw that she was about the same age as Phineas Carter. It was a long shot, but I figured what the hell. I dialed the number.

There were babies crying in the background, and the woman who answered didn't speak English.

"Pamela Wade," I said, trying to enunciate every syllable slowly and clearly.

"*Oh! Pamelita. Un momentito, por favor.*"

Approximately *un momentito* later, Pamela Wade came to the phone.

"Sorry," she said. "That was my neighbor. She was expecting a call from her husband."

"I'm looking for the Pamela Wade who was involved with a man named Phineas Carter," I said.

"Phin's dead. What do you want?"

So it was her. On the Tone of Politeness meter, where zero is receptionist-pleasant and ten is flat-out hostile, Pamela's voice had gone from a one to a four.

"I was hired to investigate his murder," I said. "I just wanted to ask you a few questions."

"Who hired you?"

"His daughter."

"Now I know you're full of shit. Phin didn't have a daughter."

I explained the situation, told her about the research I'd done. "He might not have told you about it, but he definitely had a daughter. She has a terminal illness, and she'd wanted to meet him before she dies."

"OK. Whatever. So what can I help you with?"

The dying client thing doesn't work every time.

"I've read everything that was printed in the newspapers," I said. "But I don't have access to the police files. I was just wondering—"

"So you want all the gory details? Well, today's your lucky day, then, Mr. Colt, because I'm the one who found him. He was shot once, through the forehead at close range. There was blood and bone and brain tissue splattered on the wall behind him. The police retrieved a bullet, a single thirty-eight slug, but they never found the weapon it was fired from. There was no sign of forced entry, and they couldn't find a single shred of forensic evidence. Not even a fingerprint. Whoever killed him did it execution-style. Apparently he'd been on his knees with his hands behind his head. No signs of a struggle, no evidence whatsoever that he'd put up a fight."

The needle on the Tone of Politeness meter had crept to a five: edgy. The colicky kids and I were doing our best to push it into the red zone.

I decided to cut to the chase. "Was he involved in the use or sale of illegal drugs?" I asked.

"Are you kidding? Phin didn't even drink. He'd been sober for over six years. No drugs, no booze, nothing."

I wanted to believe her, but addicts lie. Addicts lie, and they hide things. It's what they do. Pamela Wade was under no obligation to talk to me, so I figured she was telling me what she *thought* to be the truth. She had no reason to lie. At any given moment she could have said "fuck you" and hung up and that would have been it. She thought she was telling me the truth, but Phin might have hidden some things from her. He might have been into some things she didn't know about. She said he'd been sober for six years, but I still wasn't convinced.

"How long had the two of you been together?" I asked.

"We started dating six years ago. We actually met in rehab. I'd been living with him for the last five, and we'd been married for the last three. I think I would have known if he was using or selling drugs. I'm telling you, the man was a teetotaler. He was into organic foods and herbs and vitamins and all that. He rarely even drank a cup of coffee."

"You were married?" I asked.

"Yeah. We took a trip to Vegas one time and…yeah. We had the piece of paper, but we really didn't advertise it much. I never changed my name or anything."

"Do you use illegal drugs?" I asked.

It caught her off guard. Silence, and then, "I might take a hit on a joint every now and then, but nothing any harder than that. Not that it's any of your business. And it's not like I do it every day. Just occasionally, if I'm at a party or whatever. Phin's murder had nothing to do with drugs, Mr.—what did you say your name was?"

"Colt."

"Mr. Colt. I was in love with Phineas T. Carter, and we were together practically all the time. I told the cops, and I'll tell you. He was straight as an arrow."

"What kind of work did he do?" I asked.

"He was self-employed. He did some carpentry, light plumbing, and electrical. You know, handyman kind of stuff. He did all right."

"Did he have any enemies? Were any of his customers pissed off about anything?"

"Everyone loved Phin," she said. "And his work was first-rate. He would get the occasional complaint now and then, like you do in any kind of business, but whenever that happened he would always go back and fix whatever it was. At no extra charge, I might add. Phin wasn't happy until the customer was happy. And that's the way it should be. Hell, I wish more people were like him."

"Sounds like a good guy," I said.

"He was."

I was trying to dredge up something that might remotely resemble a lead, but I was running out of ideas.

"Did he have any hobbies?" I asked. "Golf or anything? Did he belong to any organizations? A lodge or a church or anything?"

"He played chess."

"Chess?"

"He hung out at a little grocery over on Eaton Street. He would go over there for a few hours on his days off and play chess and shoot the shit. It was basically his only social outlet. Aside from me, of course."

"What's the name of the shop?"

She told me the name of the place, and I wrote it down.

"And what about you?" I asked.

"Excuse me?"

"As a social outlet. Did you have any relatives or ex-boyfriends or anything who might have—"

"Like I said, everyone loved Phin. And all my exes were long gone by the time he was murdered."

There was a knock on my door. I looked through the peephole. It was the pizza man.

"OK," I said. "Well, I certainly appreciate your time, Ms. Wade. Would it be all right to call you again if I think of any other questions?"

"Please don't. I've given you all I have, and I'm really just trying to move on with my life."

The babies had quieted down, and Pamela's voice had eased off to a three. She sounded almost sleepy now.

"Thanks again for your time," I said. "And I'm truly sorry for your loss."

She hung up.

I answered the door and paid for my pizza. I ate two pieces and watched some television and tried to fall asleep but couldn't. Finally I put my clothes back on and walked down to the lounge. After three more drinks, Wesley West started sounding better. I bought him a shot of tequila when he went on break. We talked for a while, and I ended up leaving the bar at 4:00 a.m., when it closed.

CHAPTER SIX

Rex is still standing at the grill flipping brains, trying his best not to laugh as the other zombies pig out on the sheriff. The sheriff is still alive, convulsing on the floor, but you get the sense there is no hope for him now.

"Hey, Boomer, come here," Rex says.

The zombie named Boomer looks up. He opens his mouth, revealing one of the sheriff's eyeballs rolling around on his tongue. He closes his mouth and swallows.

"Be right there," he says.

He walks behind the counter and stands beside Rex at the griddle.

"Crack me some eggs," Rex says.

Boomer grabs a carton from the refrigerator, starts cracking them into a steel mixing bowl. Then he gets the inexplicable idea to launch one of the raw eggs at the other zombies. It lands on the top of one of their heads with a moist crack.

Boomer laughs. "Look at Grady. He's an egghead now."

Grady reaches into the open wound on the sheriff's massive belly, sticks his arm in all the way to the elbow, and emerges with the sheriff's heart in his hand.

The heart is still beating.

Grady throws it overhand like a baseball. It whizzes by Boomer's head, barely missing him, and lands on the hot cooking surface with a splattering sizzle.

"Food fight!" Boomer says.

Boomer and Rex start throwing eggs and pies and pork chops, and an assortment of other food items from the kitchen, while the other zombies throw an assortment of the redneck sheriff's internal organs…

I got up around nine and took a shower and grabbed a cup of coffee from the continental breakfast downstairs. I drove over to Eaton Street, to the store Pamela Wade had told me about.

Kenny's Organic Grocery.

From the plate-glass storefront I could see bins of fresh produce against the left wall, and two aisles of shelving straight ahead. The counter and the cash register were on the right, but the station appeared to be unmanned at the moment. A little bell jingled when I opened the door. I walked in and looked around. The apples smelled wonderful. The shelves were full of expensive things that were supposed to be good for you. Noodles made from spinach, low-sodium soups, vegan mayonnaise. Stuff like that. I could see right away that it would cost a small fortune to shop there all the time. It seemed like a racket to me, but maybe there was something to it. I wondered if I would live longer if I choked down a handful of goji berries with my next chimichanga.

"Can I help you?"

A woman appeared at the end of the aisle. She had very long black hair accented with the occasional strand of gray. She wore a blue dress with a flower print on it and a lace collar. Stout leather shoes from the *Little House on the Prairie* collection.

"Do people play chess here?" I asked.

"We have a little café in the back. You're welcome to check it out if you want to."

"Thanks. I think I will."

"My name's Barbara. Let me know if you need anything. I'll be around."

"OK."

There were two doors at the back of the grocery. One of them said *Restrooms* and the other said *To Café*. I opened the latter and walked in. There was a lunch counter on the left, and four tables on the right. Four deuces, as restaurant people tend to call tables for two. Every one of them had a black-and-white chessboard painted onto the solid wood top. Three of the tables were vacant, but a couple of guys sat at the one farthest from the door I'd come in through. They were older guys. Retirement age, maybe. One with thick white hair and the other completely bald. They were both intensely focused on the game in front of them. I sat at the counter and ordered a cup of coffee and watched them play. When Baldy took Whitey's queen, I figured it might be a decent time to interrupt.

"Good move," I said.

They glanced my way.

"I'll beat his ass without a queen," Whitey said. "I've done it before."

I slid down from my stool and walked over to the table. "Did y'all know a guy named Phineas Carter who used to come in here and play sometimes?"

"Who are you?" Baldy asked.

"Just an old friend."

"Phin got killed, man. Someone came into his house and shot him in the head."

"I know. So tell me, you guys ever play for money?"

Whitey laughed. "We always play for money."

"Did Phin play for money?" I asked.

"Of course," Whitey said. "What are you getting at?"

"I'm not a chess player," I said. "But I imagine it's not all that different from any other sort of gambling. Guys get pissed off sometimes when they lose, especially when substantial amounts of money are involved."

"You trying to say someone killed Phineas Carter over a chess game?" Baldy asked.

"I'm not saying anything. Just wondering if it could have happened."

"Chess is a thoughtful game," Whitey said. "Played by thoughtful people. It doesn't get rowdy, the way poker does sometimes, and it's not a game of chance. You win at chess because you outthink the other guy."

"Strictly skill," Baldy said. "We play for five dollars a game, and I never saw Phineas Carter play for any more than that. Nobody's going to kill anyone over five or ten bucks."

"And people who play chess at this level aren't like that anyway," Whitey said. "I don't know who you are, but you're barking up the wrong tree."

"I guess so," I said. "Thanks for your time. I'll let you get on with your game."

I walked back to the counter and sat on my stool.

"You want another cup?" The guy minding the café looked to be in his mid-fifties. He had curly salt-and-pepper hair, and a thick black mustache. He wore jeans and a red T-shirt and a white chef's apron.

"Sure," I said. "Are you Kenny, by any chance?"

"That would be me. Head cook and bottle washer."

"And the lady watching the grocery store up front. Is that your wife?"

"For twenty-six years," he said.

"Ken and Barbie?"

He chuckled. "I know. We hear the jokes all the time. For twenty-six years we've been hearing them."

He brought the coffeepot and filled my cup.

"Did you know a guy named Phineas Carter who used to come in here?" I asked.

"Yeah, I remember him. He was a good chess player. Hardly ever lost. In fact, I played him myself a few times. It was a real shock to the community when his wife found him shot to death in their apartment. That was before all this Zombie shit we're dealing with now. It was a real shock."

"Did you ever know of anybody who might have had it in for him?"

"Are you a cop?"

"No."

"There was a cop in here asking me the same questions, soon after Phin was killed. Guy named Sullivan."

"I'm not a cop," I said.

"Anyway, no, Phineas Carter didn't have an enemy in the world. Not that I know of. He was always smiling and cutting up. He was the kind of guy everyone liked to be around."

Yet someone drilled a .38 slug into his brain, I thought.

My cup was still half-full, but I'd had enough. And, I'd heard enough.

"Good coffee," I said. "Thanks a lot."

I paid, and then walked back through the grocery to the exit. The door jingled again when I pushed it open to walk out.

"Come back and see us," Barbara said.

I smiled and waved and left the store. I doubted I would be back.

I tried to call Alison Palmer, the woman who owned the condo where Phineas T. Carter had been murdered. According to Darcy, the real-estate agent, Alison was living at the place now. I wanted to see if she knew anything about Phin, maybe some things Pamela Wade had left out. Phin had to have been into something shady. If it wasn't drugs, it was something else. People don't just waltz into your house and blow your brains out with a .38 for no reason. Not usually.

According to the newspapers, there had been nothing missing from the apartment, not even the dead man's wallet. So that ruled burglary out. There were no signs of forced entry, which told me the assailant was someone Phin knew. Phin had opened the door for the perpetrator, and had willingly allowed him to come in.

Assuming it was a *him*. It could have been a female, but I didn't think so. Most of your hard-core cold-blooded assassins are guys. That's just the way it is.

There were no signs of a struggle, which told me Phin didn't necessarily think he was going to die. That was important. When you're on your knees with your hands behind your head and someone presses the barrel of a revolver against your forehead, nine times out of ten you're going to think death is imminent. Nine times out of ten you're going to do whatever you can to stop it. You're going to hit the gunman in the balls or try to grab the gun or something. Phin wasn't helpless. He hadn't been tied up or anything. If he had thought he was going to die, he would have done something.

But he didn't do anything. There were no signs of a struggle.

Which told me the guy with the gun was probably trying to get some kind of information from Phin.

My first thought had been drugs, because of Phin's alleged smuggling history, but it could have been something else. Gambling, prostitution, blackmail. I'd pretty much ruled chess out, but it could have been anything else. Most likely something illegal that involved large sums of money. I hadn't pressed Pamela Wade on any of it. If Phin had been into something bad, Pamela might have been into it with him. I didn't want to spook her. I didn't want her to leave Fort Lauderdale, or maybe even leave the country.

She had been cleared of the murder charge, but I wondered how far the police had gone with their investigation into her personal life. Probably not as far as I wanted to go. I knew her address now, and I planned to drive up to Lauderdale and follow her around for a while. If she had any dealings with the wrong kinds of people, I would find out about it sooner or later. And if she did, the people she was involved with might be the same people Phin had been involved with.

I planned on driving up to Lauderdale, but today I wanted to talk to Alison Palmer. I tried calling several times, left several messages on voice mail, and finally decided to ride over there. If she was home, maybe I could get her to talk to me. If she wasn't home, I could wait there until she came back.

She wasn't home.

It was a fairly large complex, three buildings, three stories each. Weathered cedar lap siding with black architectural shingles. Balconies with folding chairs and barbecue grills. Alison's unit was in the middle building, on the second floor. I walked up there and knocked and rang the bell and knocked again, but nobody answered.

I walked back to the parking lot, sat in the hot Jimmy, and waited.

And waited.

A spot by a tree finally opened up, so I pulled over there and parked in the shade. It was twenty degrees cooler. It was like paradise compared to where I'd been before. My throat was as dry as sandpaper, and I had a headache from drinking too much whiskey at the hotel lounge last night. I thought about driving down the road and buying a bottle of water and some aspirin, but I didn't want to risk losing my shady parking place.

I sat there for another hour and was about to pass out from dehydration when a black Ford Ranger with a matching topper pulled up in front of Alison's building. A man got out carrying a bag of groceries in one hand and a six-pack of beer in the other. Maybe he was one of Alison's neighbors. Maybe he could give me an idea of what time she might be home.

I climbed out of the Jimmy and walked toward Alison's building. By the time I made it to the second-floor landing, the guy from the pickup truck was sticking a key in Alison's door.

"Hi there," I said, catching him before he turned the key and opened the door.

I startled him. He turned with a jerk. "Can I help you?" he said.

"My name is Nicholas Colt. I'm a private investigator. I'm looking for a woman named Alison Palmer."

"May I ask why?" he said.

I guessed him to be in his early thirties. Medium build, long brown hair tied back in a ponytail. He wore denim shorts and a sleeveless T-shirt and Converse All Stars. Red ones. I'd owned a pair just like them forty years ago.

"I'm investigating the murder of a man named Phineas T. Carter," I said. "I understand Ms. Palmer owns the condominium where it happened."

"The police—"

"I'm sorry," I said. "What was your name?"

"Robbie Asbury. I'm Alison's husband."

"OK. Now what were you saying about the police?"

"Yeah, the cops already went over everything with her, and of course all the evidence is long gone. The place was a mess. The carpeting in the living room had to be replaced, along with the Sheetrock on one whole wall."

"I'd still like to talk to her," I said. "Would you happen to know what time she might be home?"

"She's here now," he said. "I parked my car right beside hers."

"Nobody answered when I knocked," I said.

"She worked last night, so she might still be asleep. Let me just go in and check."

"OK."

He turned the key and opened the latch, picked up his six-pack and groceries from where he'd set them on the stoop, walked inside, and shut the door.

Thirty seconds later I heard him scream.

CHAPTER SEVEN

Robbie Asbury came running out the door with his hand over his mouth. He leaned over the second-floor railing and puked into the bushes below.

He was crying. "She's dead," he said. "Oh my god, Alison's dead."

I walked into the apartment, making sure I didn't touch anything. It felt as though a giant electrified paintbrush swiped a chill from the base of my spine to the top of my scalp. Alison Palmer was on the bedroom floor, on her back, staring blankly at the ceiling. There was a horizontal incision on her forehead, about two inches above her eyebrows. It was crusted with dried blood. I imagined that the cut went all the way around, but most of it was hidden by her frizzy brown hair. I imagined that the top of her skull had been gently lifted and then glued back down once the contents had been removed.

The sight of her lying there was too much. I felt my stomach lurch, sure for a moment that I was going to join Robbie Asbury at the railing.

I pulled out my cell phone and dialed 911.

"Emergency Services," a female voice said. "Is this an actual emergency?"

"The Zombie," I said. I could barely speak.

"Excuse me?"

"There's been a murder," I said.

"Where are you calling from, sir?"

I tried to think. It finally came to me. I told her the address. "There's been a murder," I said again.

"Sir, I want you to stay on the line until someone gets there. OK?"

"OK."

"Are you inside the apartment right now?"

"Yes."

"Can you please describe what's happening there right now?"

"Nothing's happening," I said. "There's a body on the floor."

"Is anyone else there with you? Are you in any immediate danger?"

"No."

"Is the victim male or female?"

"Female."

"I want you to look closely at her chest. Is she breathing?"

"She's dead."

"I want you to press two fingers against the side of her neck and feel for a pulse."

"She's *dead*," I shouted. "You understand that? She's not breathing and she doesn't have a pulse. I know this for a fact. I know it because she doesn't have a goddamn brain."

"Sir, I need you to try to remain calm. Did you feel for a pulse like I asked you to?"

I hung up. I knew what was coming next. She was going to tell me to start performing CPR until rescue arrived. She was going to tell me to give Alison Palmer mouth-to-mouth and pump on her chest with the butt of my hand. And if I thought there was the slightest possibility of any of that helping, I would have done it. But there was no point in putting my mouth on those cold blue lips and forcing air into those breathless lungs. There was no point in cracking those stiffening ribs in an effort to revive that bloodless heart.

Alison Palmer was dead.

I walked out of the apartment. Robbie Asbury was still heaving over the rail and crying hysterically.

I wanted to say something to him. Try to soothe him. But what do you say in a case like that?

Everything's going to be all right.

Everything wasn't going to be all right. Everything was incredibly fucked-up, and there was no indication that everything was not going to be incredibly fucked-up anytime soon.

I decided not to say anything. I walked down the stairs and over to my car. I leaned on the hood with my face in my hands. I had the shakes. Like an alcoholic. I couldn't control it. The ghastly image of Alison Palmer's brainless corpse had been indelibly etched into my consciousness, like a burn scar from a branding iron. I tried to think about something else, but I couldn't. It was going to be with me for a long, long time.

The Zombie.

I joked around sometimes, but terrifying nightmares plagued me for months after watching *Time Traveling Zombie Bikers from Darkest Hell.* I would wake up in a panic, wanting to run but paralyzed with fear, certain that one of those clammy fuckers was under my bed. Certain that one of them was going to crack my skull like a walnut and feast on my twelve-year-old brain.

I joked around sometimes to help relieve my own anxiety.

I still have the nightmares occasionally, and to this day I refuse to watch any movie or television show that deals with zombies. Even the ones that are supposed to be funny. I can't watch them. They do something to me. It's almost like my Kryptonite or something.

There's a word for my condition. Kinemortophobia. The fear of zombies. I looked it up one time. As phobias go, it's a pretty ridiculous one. I know that.

I've never admitted my irrational fear of the walking dead to anyone. I'm sure they would just laugh. It's like saying you're afraid of ghosts or vampires or something. Those things aren't real. *Zombies* aren't real. At least the pop culture ones aren't. Apparently the myth evolved from some sort of Haitian and West African voodoo practices, where a variety of chemicals throw victims into a perpetual dazed state. But the creatures we normally think of as zombies, the shambling dullards in movies like *Night of the Living Dead* and *Flesh Eating Mothers*, are about as real as Donald Duck.

Yet they strike a fear in me that is palpable.

Of course, I knew the serial killer terrorizing the southeastern United States from the Keys to Savannah wasn't really a zombie. I knew he was just some sick, depraved asshole with a flare for the dramatic. The brains were just trophies for him. Like some serial killers take a piece of jewelry from their victims or an article of clothing or some other memento. Something to remember the occasion by, something to get off on again and again in the future. The Zombie probably kept his victims' brains in Ziploc bags in the freezer. Or maybe he immortalized them in blocks of Lucite. Whatever. I knew the motherfucker wasn't a real zombie.

But seeing Alison Palmer lying there with that incision across her forehead did something to me. It shook me somewhere deep. It rattled me at the core.

I'm not sure how much time elapsed, but when I looked up, there was a police cruiser parked at the sidewalk in front of Alison's building. Blue lights flashing. There was one officer, still in the driver's seat. I walked over there as he was getting out. He saw me coming.

"Did someone call nine-one-one?" he said.

"I did. There's a dead woman up on the second floor."

"You found her?"

"Her husband found her," I said. "Then I went in and saw her."

"Are you one of their neighbors?"

"Just a concerned citizen."

"You want to walk up there with me?" the officer said.

"I'd just as soon wait down here. Her husband can show you in."

"That your Chevy Blazer over there?"

"It's a GMC Jimmy. Yeah, it's mine."

He pulled out a notepad and wrote down the tag number. "Don't go anywhere," he said. "We're going to want to talk to you."

He put the notepad back in his pocket and followed the sidewalk to the stairs. I took a deep breath, walked back to my car, sat inside and waited.

An ambulance came and the EMS guys bolted up the stairwell carrying nylon cases that said *TRAUMA ONE.* A few minutes later two more police cars came and two more uniformed officers climbed to the second floor.

I called Juliet, but got voice mail. I looked at my watch. 3:47. She was at work. I called the number to her unit at the hospital. The clerk said Juliet was busy with a patient, but if I wanted to hold she could probably talk to me in a few minutes. I said I would try back later. I needed to talk to someone. I needed to talk to Joe Crawford, my best friend since sixth grade. But I couldn't. A little over a year ago, an insane billionaire sadist named Malden Zephauser had used real live human beings in a demented version of the video game Snuff Tag 9, and Joe had gotten sucked into it because of me. I couldn't call my best friend since sixth grade because my best friend since sixth grade was dead.

A few minutes after four, an unmarked Camaro rolled in and parked behind the three police cruisers. The car looked brand new.

It was a convertible, but the top was up. Heavy tint on the windows. A man wearing gray pants and a white dress shirt got out. He had a shiny gold badge hooked to the front of his belt and a flat black Glock holstered to the side. Slicked-back hair, wraparound shades. He was slim and trim, and he moved with the slow, nonchalant grace and confidence of a tiger on the prowl. He followed the same path the others had taken to the second level.

I tried Juliet again. This time she was at the nurses' station, and the clerk transferred the call to her desk.

"Hi there," she said. "How's it going?"

"Not good," I said. "Not good at all."

I told her about everything that had happened.

"You should come home now, Nicholas. It's just not worth it."

"I told Wanda I would try to find out who killed her father, so that's what I'm going to do. I can't just give up after one day."

"You can, and you should. You don't owe that woman anything. Give her back the ten thousand dollars and be done with it. She can find somebody else to look for her father's killer."

It was tempting, especially with my phobia gnawing its way deeper and deeper into my head. But quitting just felt like the wrong thing to do. Like a giant backward leap into the infernal regions of uselessness.

"I'm going to keep working on it, Jules. At least for a few more days. That is, if I don't get arrested."

"What do you mean?"

"I walked into Alison Palmer's apartment and saw her lying on the floor dead. The police want to talk to me. They're going to want to know what I was doing here in the first place. If I tell them the truth, they're going to want to see my PI license."

"And you don't have a PI license."

"Exactly."

"And you're on probation."

"Exactly."

"So what are you going to tell them?"

"I don't know. I—"

I stopped talking mid-sentence, because I couldn't believe my eyes.

There was short pause, and then Juliet said, "Nicholas?"

"I'm here. I think I just found a way out of this. I'll call you back in a little while."

We said good-bye, and I climbed out of my car and rushed over to the other side of the parking lot.

CHAPTER EIGHT

While I was talking to my wife, Wesley West had steered his old Taurus station wagon into the lot. Wesley West was the guy who'd been singing and playing acoustic guitar at the hotel lounge last night. The one with the beret and the dark glasses. The one who wasn't very good.

He was carrying half a gallon of ice cream in a translucent plastic grocery bag. Breyers. I couldn't make out the flavor. He squinted as I approached him, and then smiled when he recognized me.

"Nicholas Colt. Hey, man. What brings you out this way?"

"I came to see you," I said.

"How did you know where I live?"

"You told me. Remember?"

Wesley and I had talked last night during his breaks, and I had bought him several beers and several shots of tequila. At four o'clock when the place closed, he was at least as drunk as I was.

He tugged on his goatee. "If you say so," he said.

"Yeah, I was going to show you some things on the guitar. I can't believe you don't remember."

"Well, my memory's not what it used to be. Especially after a tequila night. Come on up and we'll pick a little."

Score. My lucky day.

"As it turns out, I'm going to have to take a rain check," I said.

I told him about what had happened, about Alison Palmer being murdered. I told him about the incision across her forehead.

He stared in the direction of Alison's building. "Great God almighty," he said. "Are you sure it was The Zombie? Here?"

"It looks that way," I said. "Listen, if the cops ask, I came to the complex to see you. OK?"

"Sure, Nicholas. Sure. Damn. I can't believe this shit, man. The fucking Zombie. Right here in my backyard."

"I'll let you go before your ice cream melts," I said. "You playing at the lounge again tonight?"

"Yeah."

"I'll probably see you there."

"OK."

He walked away shaking his head.

I walked back to the Jimmy, and a few minutes later the detective who'd driven up in the Camaro came over and asked if I would mind answering a few questions.

"I wouldn't mind at all," I said. "I'd be happy to help in any way I can."

"Let's walk over to my car," he said.

"OK."

He introduced himself. Detective Craig P. Sullivan, Monroe County Sheriff's Office, Homicide Investigations Unit. I remembered the name Sullivan from Kenny at the granola chess café. His friends called him Sully. Nobody told me that. It was a guess. Almost every cop in the universe named Sullivan had friends who shortened it to Sully. It was practically a rule. We walked over to his car. He opened the passenger's side door for me, and I climbed in. He shut the door, walked around, took a seat behind the wheel.

"Nice ride," I said.

"Thanks. For the record, your name is Nicholas Colt. Is that correct?"

"That's right. How did you know my name?"

I'd told Robbie Asbury my name and my purpose for being there, but I was hoping that all of the emotional trauma he was going through had shaken it out of him.

"One of the patrolmen ran your tags," Sullivan said. "Can I see your driver's license, please?"

I handed him my license.

"Clay County," he said. "What brings you down to Key West?"

"I'm on vacation."

"You're also on probation. Want to tell me about that?"

"Possession of heroin," I said. "I had a problem with it, but I've been clean for over a year."

He handed my license back. "So what was the nature of your business with Ms. Palmer this afternoon?"

"I didn't have any business with her," I said. "I was here to see someone else."

He looked at his notes. "I talked to a man who claims to be her husband, a Mr. Robert Asbury. Different last names, but a lot of women are doing that these days. He was under the impression that you had come here to see her."

"Then he was under the wrong impression. He must have misunderstood."

"I see. So you were here to visit someone else, but you were knocking on Ms. Palmer's door. Out of all the doors in this condominium complex, you picked the one with a dead person behind it. That's really an amazing coincidence, Mr. Colt. For some reason, I'm having a hard time wrapping my head around that."

"It happens," I said.

He looked doubtful. He wrote something in his notebook.

"I was here to see a man named Wesley West," I said. "I just met him last night. I must have written down the wrong apartment number."

"What apartment does Wesley West live in?"

"I don't know. I never made it there."

"We'll check up on that," Sullivan said.

"OK."

"So tell me exactly what happened, Mr. Colt. Tell me exactly how it came to be that you walked into Alison Palmer's apartment and found her dead on the floor."

It took about ten minutes for me to go through it all. He wrote everything down.

"Can I go now?" I said.

"Did you know we've been dealing with a serial killer down here, Mr. Colt?"

"The Zombie," I said. "I've heard about it."

"Pretty creepy, wouldn't you say?"

"Yeah. Creepy as hell."

Detective Sullivan took his sunglasses off. His eyes were blue and bloodshot. "Where are you staying?" he said.

I told him the name of the hotel and the room number.

"Plan on being there a few more days?" he said.

"Yeah."

"Good. We might need to talk to you again."

"That's fine. Like I said, I would be happy to help in any way I can."

He handed me a business card. "Call me if you think of anything else that might me pertinent."

"OK. I will."

"Have a good night, Mr. Colt."

I opened the door and started to climb out.

"Oh," he said. "Could you give me your cell phone number, just in case I can't reach you at the hotel?"

I gave him the number, happy to get out of that car and put some distance between myself and the law.

CHAPTER NINE

If the police had found out I was there working as a private investigator, I would have been carted off to jail. I would have gone directly to jail. I would not have passed *GO*, and I would not have collected $200.

Under normal circumstances, I probably would have been slapped with a hefty fine for unlawfully performing the duties of a licensed professional. But these weren't normal circumstances. I'd lost my PI license because of a narcotics conviction. I was still on probation.

And with a murder case, they could have charged me with all kinds of things. Obstruction of justice came to mind. Tampering with evidence. Police detectives never seem to have a sense of humor about that stuff. Go figure.

Depending on what they charged me with and what kind of mood the judge was in, I could have served some real prison time. I'd dodged a bullet big-time, thanks to Wesley West. I planned on dropping an extra ten in his tip jar tonight.

I left the parking lot of the condo complex and stopped at the nearest McDonald's. I bought two Big Macs and a large order of fries and a Sprite. The Sprite came in a cup you could have used for a mop bucket.

I ate both the burgers and half the fries and sucked the soda down to the ice. It was my first meal of the day. It hit the spot.

I left McDonald's and drove back to the hotel.

I turned on the television and stared at it with the sound muted. It was a *Seinfeld* rerun. Jerry and Elaine were sitting on Jerry's couch talking about something. I tried to forget about Alison Palmer's ghostly pale face. I tried to forget about those dead eyes staring at the ceiling. But I couldn't.

Two murders had occurred in the same apartment. First Phineas Carter, and now Alison Palmer. The location seemed to be the only similarity, but I wondered if there was more. I wondered if there was a connection.

I called Darcy Clermont again. This time she picked up on the first ring.

"Red Parrot Realty," she said.

"Darcy, this is Nicholas Colt."

"Oh, did you find something you're interested in?"

"I have bad news," I said. "Alison Palmer is dead. She was murdered in her apartment earlier today."

"What? I can't believe that. I was just talking to her yesterday. Surely there must be some—"

"It's true," I said. "I was there. I saw her. I'm sure it will be on the news later."

"Oh my god."

The timbre of Darcy's voice told me she was on the verge of breaking down.

"I know it's a shock," I said. "I don't want to sound insensitive, but I was wondering if I could ask you a couple of questions."

"About Alison?"

"Yes. Like I told you before, I'm working for Phineas Carter's daughter, and I was wondering if there might be a connection between the two murders."

"Was Alison killed the same way?"

"No," I said. "It looks like that serial killer got her. The Zombie."

That was it. Darcy started sobbing then. It took her a minute to regain her composure.

"I'm sorry," she said.

"It's all right. I understand. I can call back later if you want. Or tomorrow."

"Let me just grab a Kleenex. Hold on a second."

I held on a second. Darcy came back sniffling, but her voice seemed a little steadier.

"I don't understand," she said. "What would be the connection between the two killings?"

"The location," I said. "It just seems like an incredible coincidence. And maybe that's all it is. Maybe the two murders aren't connected at all, but I want to make sure."

"OK. So what did you want to ask me?"

"First of all, I have a confession to make. I'm not exactly current on my PI paperwork, so if the police come around again to question you—"

"You don't want them to know you're working on the case?"

"Right."

"I can't make any promises," she said. "If I have to go to court, for example, I won't perjure myself for you or anyone else. But if they don't ask, I won't tell. That's the best I can do."

"Fair enough," I said. "OK, the first thing I wanted to know was why Alison subleased her condo to Phineas Carter in the first place?"

"Alison was a nurse. You knew that, right?"

"No, I didn't."

"Well, she took a job with a traveling nurse company. She wanted to see the country, especially out West. Colorado, Wyoming,

Montana. She wanted to travel around for a while, and that's why she subleased her place."

"So did she go to all those places?"

"No. Actually, she only got as far as St. Augustine."

"I'm confused," I said.

"She took a twelve-week assignment in St. Augustine while she was waiting for her Colorado nursing license to be processed. In the meantime—"

"Wait," I said. "Why the hurry? Why didn't she just stay in her condo while she was waiting for all the out-of-state paperwork to clear?"

Silence.

"There was a reason for that," Darcy said. "But I'm not at liberty to discuss it."

"With all due respect, Alison Palmer is dead. I don't see how—"

"There are other people involved. It's complicated, Mr. Colt. I just don't want to be the one to open that can of worms."

"The person or people you're protecting might be responsible for Alison's death," I said. "Or Phin's. Or both. You need to think about that."

More silence.

"I don't want to talk about it over the phone," she said. "Would it be possible for us to meet in person?"

"Certainly," I said. "How about tonight?"

"I can't tonight. In the morning. Can you meet me somewhere in the morning?"

"Sure. There's a diner on Truman Avenue. I'll buy you breakfast."

"I know the place," she said. "Is eight too early?"

"Perfect. I'll see you there."

"How will I be able to find you?"

"I'll be the guy in the John Fogerty T-shirt sitting at the counter drinking coffee."

"OK."

I sat there and watched *Seinfeld* for a few more minutes with the volume down. I kept expecting Kramer to bust in on Jerry and Elaine, but he never did.

After a while I took a shower and got dressed and walked down to the lounge.

CHAPTER TEN

I ordered an Old Fitz on the rocks and took it to a table. Wesley West was singing "Ain't No Sunshine When She's Gone" with about as much soul as a cupcake. There were twenty or so people in the bar, mostly middle-aged couples. Not a bad little crowd for a Monday night. Most of the men were drinking imported beers, and most of the women were drinking martinis. That's the way it seemed at a glance, anyway. Some of the martinis were tinted pink or green or purple. Under the barroom lights they looked like something from an episode of *Star Trek*.

When the song was over, Wesley said, "We have a distinguished guest in the audience tonight, ladies and gentlemen. I'm sure a lot of you remember the band Colt Forty-Five. They had a slew of hits back in the eighties, and their lead guitar player is sitting right over here having a cocktail. Maybe we can coax him up to the stage to play one. How about it? Let's give it up for Mr. Nicholas Colt!"

The twenty or so people applauded, and one of the more inebriated gentlemen sitting at the bar even started whistling.

I raised my palm and shook my head. There was no way I was getting up there. I hadn't played a lick since a tripped-out idiot up in Tennessee stomped my left hand with the heel of his boot. I hadn't played a lick because I couldn't. My fingers didn't work right anymore.

"Are you sure?" Wesley said, responding to my negative gestures.

I nodded. I was sure.

There was a collective *Aw* from the crowd, but they got over it soon enough. None of them came over and asked me for my autograph, or even offered to buy me a drink. Wesley jumped back in with a slow song called "Always and Forever," and a bunch of them got up to dance. After that, Wesley took a break.

I reminded myself I owed the guy. He had promised to vouch for me if anyone asked about my presence at the apartment complex. I followed him to the bar, where he was ordering a mug of draft.

"Whatever he wants is on me for the rest of the night," I said to the bartender. "Just add it to my tab."

"Well thank you, Nicholas," Wesley said. "Mind if I join you at your table?"

I waited for the bartender to fix me another drink, and then we walked back to the table together. We sat facing each other.

"You sound good tonight," I lied.

"Thanks. Yeah, you know, some nights it just flows. Tonight's one of those nights. How come you didn't want to come up and play one?"

"My hand got busted up a while back," I said. "I don't play anymore."

"But I thought that's why you were coming over to my house. So we could pick and grin a little."

"I mean I don't play anymore in public," I said, trying to cover the lie I'd told him at the complex. What a tangled web we weave, my grandmother would have said.

Wesley took a long pull on his beer. "Sorry to hear that," he said. "But I'd still like to jam a bit over at my place sometime. You know, if you're up for it. How about Wednesday night?"

"You're not playing here?" I said.

"No, I just play here on Sunday and Monday. Then I have another regular gig on Saturday. On my nights off I go out on Duval Street and play for tips sometimes, but I was planning on staying in Wednesday. So how about it?"

I didn't want to go to Wesley West's apartment, but I was afraid to say no. Afraid he might not cover for me if the cops came back around asking questions. All I needed was Detective Craig P. Sullivan hassling me about my PI license.

"All right," I said. "We'll do it Wednesday night."

CHAPTER ELEVEN

Hard rock guitars scream and psychedelic colors swirl, signaling that the time-traveling zombie bikers from darkest hell are traveling to a different time period. As the frame settles into focus, the living-dead motorcycle gang speeds down a seemingly endless dusty dirt road. They come to a fork and follow a wooden sign that says Dodge City.

They ride on and on. Finally, they stop beside a dead tree on a hill. Hundreds of cows are grazing in the valley below.

Rex and Boomer climb off their bikes.

"I'm almost out of gas," Boomer says.

"Me too," says Rex.

"Well, let's go steal some gasoline, man."

"It's eighteen forty-two, dumbass. There's no such thing as fucking gasoline."

"What the hell we doing in eighteen forty-two?" Boomer says.

"I miscalculated, that's all."

"And I'm the dumbass?"

Rex backhands Boomer across the face. Part of Boomer's right ear falls off.

"Fuck you, Boomer."

Green slime oozes from the wound on Boomer's ear. "Well, shit, man, let's just ride into another time," he says.

"You know the rules. Once we choose a time period, we have to stay there for at least twenty-four hours."

"Oh yeah. I forgot. So what the hell we gonna do?"

"I reckon we're going to get ourselves some horses and ride to town," Rex says. "'Cause I don't know about you, but I'm hungry."

"More brains! More brains!" the other zombies chant in unison.

They all follow Rex down the hill...

Tuesday morning I got to the diner at 7:48. I sat at the counter, ordered a cup of coffee, read an abandoned copy of the *Wall Street Journal.* At 8:12 a female voice from behind me said, "Are you Nicholas Colt?"

I swiveled on the stool and faced her. "I am," I said.

"Sorry I'm late."

"No problem. Want to sit at a table?"

"Yes."

The hostess led us to a booth by the front windows. Darcy Clermont looked to be in her mid to late fifties. She wore a teal business suit and a white blouse. Her hair was dyed, but it was a good job. She was an attractive woman. Fit, medium height. I felt underdressed in black jeans and a tour T-shirt.

A waitress came and asked if we wanted coffee. Her nametag said Molly. I let her refill my cup, and Darcy ordered a glass of orange juice. Darcy's eyes were red and puffy, as though she might have been crying before she came in.

"I have to be back at the office at nine," Darcy said. "So I won't have time for breakfast after all. Sorry."

"I usually just have coffee for breakfast anyway," I said. "So, since you're short on time, maybe we could just—"

"Get right to the point," she said, finishing my thought. "Alison Palmer was trying to get away from someone. That's why she subleased her condo and moved to St. Augustine while she was waiting for her Colorado nursing license. That's what you wanted to know, right?"

"Who was she trying to get away from?" I said.

"A man named Jim Ballard. She'd been in a relationship with him for a couple of years, and it ended badly."

I took a sip of coffee. "People don't usually move hundreds of miles away over a breakup," I said. "There must be more to it than that."

"Did I say it ended badly? It ended *very* badly. Jim had been drinking a lot and he got physical with her one night and pushed her around. That was it for Alison. She broke it off right away. She told him she never wanted to see him again, but he wouldn't leave her alone. He kept calling her, twenty times a day sometimes."

"There are anti-stalking laws in Florida," I said.

Molly brought the orange juice and asked if we were ready to order. I told her just the coffee and the juice. She looked disappointed. She put the ticket on the table, turned and walked away.

"I think Alison was really scared of that guy," Darcy said. "She was scared of what he might do to her, you know?"

"The two of you must have been close," I said. "Most people don't divulge that much personal information to their real estate agent."

"I guess we kind of became friends. We talked on the phone quite a bit, went out to lunch a few times. I'm a good talker, and a good listener. It's one of the reasons I can make a living selling houses."

"There's something else I'm still a little baffled about," I said. "Alison moved to St. Augustine for a twelve-week assignment while she was waiting for her Colorado license, but then she moved back here to Key West. She never went to Colorado. How come?"

Darcy dabbed at the corners of her eyes with a napkin. "This is hard for me to talk about, Mr. Colt."

"Nicholas. Please."

"This is hard for me to talk about, Nicholas. Like I said, Alison and I had become friends. I still can't believe she's gone. Just like that. Anyway, you're right. She never went to Colorado, or anywhere else. While she was in St. Augustine, she met another man. A guy named Robbie Asbury."

"I met him," I said. "At the apartment yesterday. We kind of found her together."

"He's a drummer," Darcy said. "He was living in St. Augustine when Alison moved up there, and they met at the beach and went out a couple of times. All this happened around the same time Phineas Carter was murdered. Robbie subbed for a drummer at a club down here in Key West, and the band ended up hiring him full-time." She paused. "I'm trying to think of the name of the band. Blue Waves. That's it. Believe it or not, their former drummer plays for Alice Cooper now. Anyway, Blue Waves ended up getting a job as the house band at the club, so all of a sudden Robbie Asbury had to move down here. Alison liked Robbie a lot, so she put her traveling plans on hold and moved back into her condo. Soon after that, Robbie moved in with her, and then they got married not long ago. It was such a nice little ceremony. I'd never seen Alison so happy."

"Is Robbie still playing with the band?" I said.

"Yeah. That's his job. But I'm sure he'll have to find someone to sub for *him* while he's dealing with everything that's going on."

"I'm sure," I said. "What's the name of the club?"

"Jake's Key West Saloon. Oh, and get this. Jim Ballard hangs out there. Alison's ex. Somehow, Jim and Alison and Robbie all managed to start getting along. Which seemed kind of strange, after everything that had happened between Alison and Jim. From the way Alison talked, it was like the three of them had actually become friends."

Molly came and filled my coffee cup. She smiled and walked away.

"That is unusual," I said. "From what you told me about this Jim Ballard guy, it sounds like he was a real asshole. Like he was obsessed with Alison. Guys like that usually have a problem letting go and moving on. I just can't imagine him being very friendly toward Alison's new love interest."

"I know. It's weird. But that's what Alison said. She said Jim still comes to the club a lot, and that they all get along just fine. But it makes you wonder. I'm sure the police will want to question Jim Ballard."

"I suppose," I said. "Although the murder was obviously the work of The Zombie."

I took a sip of coffee.

"Or a copycat," I said. "You think Jim Ballard was crazy enough to saw the top of Alison's skull off and steal her brain?"

Darcy suddenly looked pale. "Excuse me," she said.

She got up and walked to the restroom.

I sat there feeling bad about what I'd said. The way I'd said it. Good old Nicholas Colt. Subtle as a jackhammer.

But there really wasn't a nice way to discuss something so gruesome. Alison Palmer's head had been opened like a can, her brain scooped out like pickled cabbage. How could you sugarcoat that? You couldn't. There was no way.

Or maybe there was a way, and the brutalities I'd faced in my own life had desensitized me too much to find it. At any rate, I felt bad, and when Darcy came back to the table I told her so.

"It's OK," she said. "It's just not fair. Alison was such a beautiful person, inside and out. A lot of people are going to miss her. I'm going to miss her."

"I appreciate you meeting me here and talking to me," I said.

She looked at her watch. "I have to go. But to answer your question, yes, I think Jim Ballard was capable of doing that to Alison. I've never met the guy, but when Alison was in the process of moving up to St. Augustine, she told me some things. Jim won a big settlement in a lawsuit a few years ago, and he hasn't worked a day since. All he does is drink, all day every day. Jim drinks a lot, and sometimes he has total blackouts. According to Alison, he never remembered physically abusing her."

"So..."

"So maybe he doesn't remember killing her."

CHAPTER TWELVE

After Darcy left, I ended up ordering a stack of pancakes and some bacon and eggs. I sent back the little tubs of whipped spread Molly brought and asked for some genuine butter. When she said they didn't have any, I told her margarine produces a chemical reaction in my bloodstream that counteracts and nullifies the therapeutic effects of my antipsychotic medications. Her jaw dropped. She hurried off and brought back half a stick of Breakstone's from the kitchen.

I thought about what Darcy had said. I didn't think it was possible for someone to forget about opening another person's skull and packing off with its contents.

But maybe it was possible.

In my younger days, there were nights when I couldn't remember how I'd gotten home, and mornings when I couldn't remember the name of the person lying beside me. Sometimes there were stains on my shirts from greasy late-night food I couldn't remember eating.

And just yesterday I'd managed to convince Wesley West that he had invited me to his apartment to play guitars.

So maybe it was possible for someone to get drunk enough to forget committing the act of murder. Thinking about it forced me to consider my own drinking habits. Maybe it was time to cut down. After this case, I told myself. Life was just a little too stressful right now to be worrying about it.

I finished breakfast, and on the way out I asked the cashier if she knew how to get to Jake's Key West Saloon. She gave me directions. I would have asked my waitress, but Molly had developed an acute case of shyness after the butter incident. I guess it made her nervous thinking about what I might do with a fork.

There were only two cars in Jake's parking lot. A black Cadillac Escalade and a silver Porsche Carrera. The tags on the Porsche said 2FAST4U. The joint either had rich clientele or rich owners. Or both. I walked up to the door. It was 9:56, and the sign said they didn't open until eleven. I cupped my hand against the glass and peeked inside. Nobody had turned the lights on yet, but a couple of neon beer signs allowed me to see the long wooden bar and the tables and chairs and the dance floor and the stage.

I walked around back, peeked over the privacy fence, saw picnic tables and tiki torches and a hut with steel shutters. There was a gate that granted access to the area, but it was locked.

I walked back to the front door and knocked, but nobody answered. I wondered if the cars in the parking lot belonged to drunks who had taken taxis home last night.

I drove two blocks to a convenience store, bought a bottle of water and a newspaper, and filled my gas tank. I went back to Jake's, found a shady spot, sipped my water and read my paper. The headline *ZOMBIE STRIKES AGAIN* was on the front page, above the fold. I read the story. It didn't tell me anything I didn't already know.

At 11:05 no other cars had pulled in. It was still just me and the Escalade and the Porsche. I got out and tried the front door again. It was still locked. I went back to my Jimmy and waited. It was getting hot, even in the shade. There wasn't much of a breeze.

At 11:16 a blond woman wearing a white visor and huge sunglasses steered a Mustang convertible into the lot and parked it beside the Porsche. The man sitting beside her gave her a short kiss and got out. He climbed into the Porsche, and both cars drove away.

It was getting hot, and I was getting pissed. The sign on the front door of Jake's Key West Saloon said they opened at eleven, so they should open at eleven. But then Key West was a pretty laid-back place. I reminded myself that opening and closing times were merely estimates at a lot of the local establishments.

I tried the front door again. Still locked. I banged on it hard. This time someone came. A skinny dark-haired man with a mustache. He twisted the knob to unlock the deadbolt.

He looked at his watch. "The girl who was supposed to open for me this morning hasn't shown up yet," he said. "I called someone else, and she's on the way, but it might be an hour before we can start serving food and drinks. Sorry."

"I knocked earlier, but—"

"I was busy back in the office."

"Are you Jake?"

"Yes. Jake Malone."

We shook hands.

"Nicholas Colt," I said. "Could I come in and talk to you for a minute?"

"About?"

"Robbie Asbury. He plays drums in the band here. I just have a few—"

"You motherfuckers don't waste any time, do you?"

"Pardon me?" I said.

"You're from the press, right? Another reporter called me on the phone earlier. What the hell? Robbie Asbury plays in the band at my bar. It doesn't mean I know his life history."

"You know his wife was murdered yesterday, right?"

"Yeah, and I know the police have a warrant for his arrest. They think he's the one who killed her. It's all they're talking about on CNN right now. How could anybody not know?"

I hadn't watched any television all morning. I hadn't even turned on the radio. So the possibility that Robbie Asbury had charges pending against him was news to me. Not that it came as a big surprise. Statistics don't lie. If you die under suspicious circumstances, odds are your wife or husband or someone else close to you did it. I hadn't heard the news about Robbie, but I didn't tell Jake that. If he wanted to think I was a reporter, then I was perfectly willing to let him think it.

"I understand you're busy," I said. "But if I could just have a few minutes of your time. I promise it won't take long."

"What news agency are you with?" he said.

"I'm a freelancer. I'm not with an agency."

"Damn. If a freelancer's here already, I guess it's only a matter of time until the vans with the satellite antennas start showing up. I don't have time for this shit, you know?"

"It's a hard time for a lot of people," I said.

"Yeah, well, forget it. I'm going to tell you the same thing I told the chick on the phone awhile ago. No comment."

He slammed the door in my face.

CHAPTER THIRTEEN

I bought two Pabst tall boys at a gas station and then parked by Starbucks so I could pick up their Wi-Fi signal. I opened my netbook, went to one of the database services I subscribe to, researched the license plate of the Porsche I saw leaving Jake's parking lot. 2FAST4U. The tags said Monroe County, so I knew the car belonged to someone local. Someone with money. Someone who for one reason or another didn't drive himself home last night.

It was a long shot, but sometimes long shots pay off. This one did not. I was hoping the car belonged to Jim Ballard. Darcy said he frequented the club, and a Porsche 911 Carrera seemed like just the kind of car a lottery winner or the recipient in a major lawsuit might splurge on. The car didn't belong to Jim Ballard. It belonged to a man named Cale Meade. I jotted his number on the back of Detective Craig P. Sullivan's business card. I called Meade, thinking he might at least know Jim Ballard or Robbie Asbury. I think I woke him up, and he wasn't especially pleasant about telling me that he didn't know either one of them. In fact, he told me, in no uncertain terms, to go straight to hell.

I sat there in front of Starbucks and drank my lunch from a brown paper bag. It had been awhile since I'd had a Pabst Blue

Ribbon. I couldn't even remember when. Probably the last time I went fishing with my friend Winston Fell. I call him Papa. He's a retired police officer, and he fishes with a bamboo fly rod he made himself. He's twenty-some years older than me and can still cast into an area the size of a bicycle tire. The PBR made me think about him. It's all he ever drinks. It made me think we should get together and go fishing soon.

I sipped on the beer and wondered what sort of evidence the police had compiled against Robbie Asbury. Whatever it was, they had put it together fast. They must have had something on file already, something from another case.

Or cases.

Was Robbie Asbury The Zombie? I didn't think so. I really didn't even think he killed his wife. The police always suspect the spouse first, and many times those suspicions turn out to be spot-on, but I'd seen Robbie come out of the apartment and puke over the second-floor railing. He had been in severe emotional distress. I would have bet my life on it. He could have been faking the tears and the tremors, but not the vomiting. I didn't think so. He could have stuck his finger down his throat like a bulimic, but there would have been no point to it. I was the only one there, and he wouldn't have bothered giving me such a performance. The Zombie's identity was still a mystery, in my opinion, and it was only a matter of time before he killed again.

Of course, I wasn't being paid to find The Zombie, but I still couldn't help thinking that Phineas Carter's murder and Alison's murder were somehow connected. Two of the most brutal crimes I'd ever heard of had occurred in the same apartment.

Different methods, but still.

The Zombie had killed Alison. I was pretty sure of that. Maybe The Zombie had killed Phineas T. Carter too. Maybe something went wrong, forcing The Zombie to deviate from his normal routine. It had happened plenty of times before, in other serial murder cases. All but one of Ted Bundy's victims had been bashed in the head with a crowbar and then strangled. Nobody knows why he changed things up that one time. It was a twelve-year-old girl named Kimberly Leach. The cause of death was never conclusive, but Bundy fried in the electric chair just the same.

If the two murders in the same condo weren't connected, it was like lightning striking twice in the same place. The odds against it were astronomical.

I thought there was probably a connection. And if there was, it ruled Robbie Asbury out. Robbie had been living in St. Augustine when Phineas Carter was killed. He was nowhere near that condominium complex. He probably didn't even know it existed at the time.

Robbie was a fugitive at the moment, but I doubted he would stay hidden for long. I had a feeling he would turn himself in soon. I needed to talk to him before that happened. Maybe he could give me some sort of insight into who killed Alison—and, if the murders were connected, some sort of insight into who killed Phin.

I telephoned Wanda Taylor, my client, and updated her on everything that had happened over the past couple of days.

"I've been watching the news," she said. "How utterly terrible. First my biological father was murdered in that apartment, and now the woman who was his landlady. It's just mind-blowingly fucked-up."

Mind-blowingly fucked-up indeed.

"I'm going to try to find Robbie Asbury," I said. "I don't have a clue where to start, other than maybe with Jim Ballard. The real-estate agent said Jim and Robbie had become friends. As unlikely as that seems."

"Are you all right on money?" Wanda said.

I wondered if she had forgotten about our arrangement. Some sort of memory loss related to her illness, maybe.

"I'm fine for now," I said. "I'm billing you for eight hours a day, even though I'm probably working more like nine or ten. Just so you know. It'll start adding up. But like we agreed before—"

"Don't worry about any of that," she said. "I just want you to work as fast as you can. Money is no object."

"If I can't find Robbie Asbury, or if I find him and nothing comes of it, I'm going to ride up to Fort Lauderdale and stake out the place where Phineas Carter's widow is staying. That's really the only other lead I have. If she's into drugs or some other illegal activity, it's a pretty safe bet Phin was too. If she's dealing with some bad people, they would be on the top of my list of suspects. If that's the case, then lightning really did strike twice, and my hunch about the two murders being connected is wrong."

"This is really turning into quite the mystery," she said. "Just keep me updated."

"I will."

"Thank you, Nicholas."

There were three James Ballards in the Key West white pages. I figured the Jim Ballard I was looking for would have an unlisted number, and I was right. None of them was him. I could have spent a few hours ferreting through search engines and databases trying to find his social security number, and from there I could have looked him up in the Monroe County Department of Motor Vehicles. But a lot of times the addresses on the DMV site aren't current, and a lot of times people get away with listing a PO box instead of a real address.

I hated to waste a bunch of time and then come up with a blank. My only other alternative was to go to the guy's hangout, sit at the bar and drink all day, and hope that he showed up.

It was a tough way to make a living, but somebody had to do it.

CHAPTER FOURTEEN

I drove back to Jake's Key West Saloon. There were several cars in the parking lot now, but still no news vans. The Escalade was gone, which meant Jake was gone. I walked in and sat at the bar.

My shirttails hid the .38 holstered on my belt.

A beautiful young woman wearing short shorts and a tank top slapped a napkin in front of me and said, "What can I get for you?" She had long brown hair and brown eyes and gold hoops in her ears.

"What kind of beer do you have?" I said.

"Bottle or draft?"

"Bottle."

She named about ten different varieties, and I chose a Pabst. It was what I'd started with, and the cans from the gas station had tasted pretty good. Rule #34 in Nicholas Colt's *Philosophy of Life*: If it ain't broke, don't fix it. Especially when it comes to liquid refreshments.

The bartender set the bottle of beer in front of me along with a frosty mug. I poured the beer into the mug, allowing it to grow a respectable head of foam. I took a sip.

"What's your name?" I said.

"Kris. Can I get you something to eat?"

"Not right now. Thanks."

I pulled out a twenty and set it on the bar.

"Be right back with your change," Kris said.

"You can keep it if you'll do me a favor," I said.

"What's that?"

"You know a guy named Jim Ballard who comes in here a lot?"

"Yeah. I know Jim."

"I'm going to go sit at that table over there and watch television for a while. If Jim comes in, would you send him my way?"

"Not a problem," she said.

She took the twenty.

Some of the tables against the wall had their own little thirteen-inch television screens, which allowed couples to sit down for a meal together without feeling the obligation to have an actual conversation. Watching TV in an eating establishment is bad enough, but the new breeds of cellular telephones everyone uses these days are like a license to be rude. I refuse to own one. I have a good old flip-top that I make calls with. I don't use it for anything else. In my office at home I have a black rotary-dial phone from the 1960s. I bought it at a thrift store for five bucks. It never drops a call, and it will last forever.

I sat at one of the tables, tuned the television to CNN. Alison's murder was the big story of the day, along with the hunt for Robbie. Of course they discussed the possibility of Robbie being The Zombie, although the police hadn't released any information to substantiate those speculations.

I sat there and sipped my beer and watched the news, amazed that I had somehow managed to get involved in all this. I thought about calling it quits. I hadn't gotten into any real trouble yet, and I hadn't spent much of Wanda's ten thousand dollars. It would have been easy to pack everything up and head back to North Florida that evening. But I didn't. Wanda wanted to find out who killed her father. She wanted to find out before she caught the bus herself, and apparently that grim day wasn't going to be too far in the future. I'd agreed to help her, so I needed to stick it out. I decided to stay in at a hundred percent until the end. It was the only attitude that was going to work. If I failed to solve Phineas Carter's murder before Wanda died, then I failed. But I had to at least try.

My cell phone trilled. I turned the volume down on the TV and answered it.

"Nicholas Colt," I said.

"Hey, it's Wesley West. Just making sure we're still on for tomorrow night."

I'd forgotten all about it. "Sure," I said. "What time?"

"Is seven OK?"

"Better make it eight."

"Cool. I think I forgot to tell you my apartment number."

He told me the number.

"I'll be there," I said.

A few minutes after I disconnected with Wesley West, a tall slender man with bushy sun-bleached hair walked over and said, "You looking for me?"

He wore a red polo, and jeans that might have been used to wipe up an oil spill. Three-day beard, sunburned nose. He could have used a few squirts of Visine.

"Are you Jim Ballard?" I said.

"Who wants to know?"

"My name is Nicholas Colt. I'm a private investigator. Can I talk to you for a few minutes?"

"About?"

"Alison Palmer and Robbie Asbury."

For some reason he glanced toward the front entrance. "Can I see your badge, or your license, or whatever it is you guys carry?"

"I must have left mine at home."

He bit his lower lip. "Let me just grab a beer real quick," he said.

He had a deep, resonant voice, but there was no emotion in it. He sounded like a TV announcer who'd taken a tranquilizer.

A couple of minutes later he came back to the table holding a bottle of Corona. He sat across from me, pushed a lime wedge into the bottle. "Vitamin C," he said. "It's good for you."

"Yeah. Keeps you from getting scurvy."

He drained half the beer in a single gulp. "That sucks about Alison Palmer," he said.

People handle grief in different ways. After John Lennon was shot, Paul McCartney initially responded to the media by saying, "Yeah, it's a drag." Or something like that. Jim's understatement regarding Alison's murder might have been in the same vein. Maybe he was still in shock.

Maybe, but I kept thinking about what Darcy had told me, about Jim's obsession with Alison and about the allegations of abuse.

"It definitely sucks," I said, trying to see if the sentiment sounded any better coming from my own mouth. It didn't.

Jim was silent for a few beats, momentarily focused on peeling the label off his beer bottle. He finally gave up on it and took another long pull.

"She used to be my girlfriend," he said.

"I know."

"Yeah? Who you been talking to?"

"People. Listen, I need to talk to Robbie Asbury before he turns himself into the police. I thought you might have some idea about his location."

"What makes you think he's going to turn himself into the police?" Jim said.

"What makes you think he won't?"

"I'm not at liberty to say. And I'm not at liberty to tell you where he is."

"But you know?"

"Maybe. Why is it so important for you to talk to him?"

"There was another murder in Alison's apartment," I said. "Almost a year ago. Guy named Phineas Carter. I'm sure you heard about it."

"Yeah, man. That was crazy. The guy was fucking executed."

"And nobody seems to know why."

"Something to do with drugs, if you ask me."

I took a sip of my Pabst Blue Ribbon. "That would be the natural assumption," I said. "But I have it on good authority that he'd been clean for a long time. Anyway, I was hired to investigate Phineas Carter's murder, and it seems like an incredible coincidence that he and Alison were killed in the same apartment. I'm just wondering if there's a link."

"Robbie didn't kill Alison. And he sure as hell didn't kill Phineas Carter."

"I know that," I said. "At least about Carter. Robbie was up in St. Augustine at the time. And I don't think he killed Alison either. I was there when he found her. He puked all over the bushes. Rattled as hell. I just want to talk to him, maybe get some insight into who might have wanted to kill his wife. Phineas Carter's killer and Alison's killer might be one and the same. If so, finding Phin's killer might be key in clearing Robbie of the charges he's facing. So really, when you get down to it, it's in his own best interest to talk to me."

"The Zombie killed Alison," Jim said. "They're saying all kinds of shit on the news. Like maybe Robbie did the copycat thing, or maybe Robbie really is the serial killer. It's all speculative bullshit. They're putting a lot of energy into finding Robbie while The Zombie roams free. Robbie Asbury is innocent."

"Then let me help him prove it," I said.

Jim clawed at the whiskers on his chin. "You're not going to turn him into the cops?" he said.

"No. But I'll recommend that he turns himself in. They'll catch him sooner or later anyway. Running from the police just looks like an admission of guilt to a jury."

"They'll never find him," Jim said. "He'll be out of the country by tomorrow."

"Then let me talk to him."

"You want to go see him? Right now?"

The abrupt offer caught me off guard. "Sometime today, for sure. Just give me an address and I'll—"

"That's not how it's going to work. You'll be riding with me. Blindfolded. And I'll need you to give me your cell phone right now. I'll bring you back here when we're done."

"I don't take rides from strangers," I said.

"Then you don't talk to Robbie Asbury. It's as simple as that."

"I could tell the police that you know where he is," I said. "They might give you a hard time."

"I could tell the police you're down here snooping around with no credentials," he said. "They might give *you* a hard time."

I didn't like it. I was going to be blindfolded and driven to an undisclosed location by someone I'd met ten minutes ago. Maybe Jim Ballard really did know where Robbie was hiding out, or maybe I'd said something to set him off. Maybe he was going to tie anchors to my feet and throw me off a bridge. Normally I would have trusted my instincts and said, hell no. Normally I would have told Jim Ballard to take a hike.

But I thought Robbie might be holding the key to both murders, and I thought this might be my only chance to talk to him. I thought Robbie might be holding the key and not even know it. Maybe he just needed to be asked the right questions.

I took a deep breath, thought about it.

I handed Jim Ballard my cell phone.

"OK," I said. "Let's go."

CHAPTER FIFTEEN

A man on a galloping horse blazes a dusty trail into town. Dodge City. The horse slows to a trot and then stops completely in front of a building that says JAIL. The rider dismounts, ties the horse to the hitching post, and walks inside.

There's a man sitting at a desk, writing something on a piece of paper. The wooden shingle hanging on the wall behind him says MACK CHILLIN, U.S. MARSHAL.

"Mack, you're not going to believe this," the rider says frantically.

"Whoa, Jeb. Just calm down a minute," Marshal Chillin says. "Now what's this all about?"

"Some fellas just walked into the bunkhouse over at Nate Smith's place and killed eight of his ranch hands. Killed them dead, took their clothes, stole their horses. Looks like they're headed towards Dodge, Mack. And these are some rough old boys."

"They're headed toward Dodge? How do you know?"

"Nate shot at them as they were riding off. Said they were traveling east."

Mack Chillin grabs his gunbelt from a hook on the wall, straps it on.

"All right, Jeb. I want you to go over to the Short Twig and round up as many men as you can. I have plenty of rifles and shotguns here.

If those fellas ride into Dodge, we're going to be ready for them. I won't be able to jail them all here, but maybe we can drive them out of town. Then I'll get a message to the army battalion over at Fort Riley."

Jeb darts out of the office and runs toward the saloon.

We see a close-up of Marshal Mack Chillin, who looks very worried now.

I followed Jim Ballard to his car, a gray Audi RS6 sedan. He pushed the button on his remote key, and the door locks chirped open and we climbed inside.

"I just need to stop at the Shell station real quick," he said.

I looked at his gas gauge. He had three-quarters of a tank.

"What for?" I said.

"I need to buy a blindfold. You think I carry one around with me all the time?"

"I was wondering."

He stopped at the Shell station, and I waited in the car while he went in. I got out for a second and pretended to stretch my legs and memorized the Audi's tag number. Jim came back out carrying two black bandannas. He tied one of them around my eyes, made sure it was secure, and then tied the other one on top of it. I couldn't see a thing.

"You have a gun?" he said.

"Yeah."

"Give it to me."

"No."

"Then get the fuck out of my car."

"Why do you want my gun?" I said.

"I don't know you from Adam, pal. You really think I'm going to trust you with a loaded pistol in my car?"

"I don't know you from Adam either."

"That's fine. We'll just go on back to Jake's."

He started backing out of the parking spot.

"All right," I said. "Take the fucking gun."

He took my .38. I heard him open the center console storage compartment. He dropped the gun in and snapped the compartment shut.

"Where are we going?" I said.

"Not far. Key West is a small island."

"He's still on Key West?"

"You'll see."

He took a left out of the parking lot and eased into traffic. The Audi was a nice car. Quiet. Steady. I planned to buy an imaginary one just like it as soon as my imaginary rich uncle stopped imaginarily breathing.

"I have a question," I said.

"OK."

"You and Alison used to go out, right? You were romantically involved for a couple of years. And from what I understand, you didn't take it very well when she broke it off."

"Nobody takes being dumped very well," Jim said.

"Some take it worse than others. From what I heard, you were practically stalking her."

"That's not true. I was just trying to get her back. Trying to tell her how sorry I was for what had happened. She wouldn't even answer her phone."

"And what did happen?" I said. "Why did she break up with you?"

"She claimed I abused her. Said I grabbed her arm and pushed her around. Shit like that. I don't remember any of it."

"But you were drinking when it happened."

"When it *allegedly* happened. Yeah."

"And you have blackouts sometimes."

"So they say. I still can't believe I would have done anything to hurt Alison. I loved her too much."

"Why would she have lied about it?" I said.

"I don't know."

We rode in silence for a few beats. "So I was just wondering," I said. "Since you were so hung up on Alison, still hung up on her when she started seeing Robbie Asbury, how was it that you and Robbie became friends? Seems like the two of you would have been enemies, if anything."

Jim made a left turn, and then a quick right.

"I guess I started seeing the whole thing with Alison for what it was," he said. "An obsession. It was eating me up. I finally just had to accept it and move on."

"Have the police talked to you about Alison's murder yet?"

"Not yet. I'm sure they'll get around to it."

"Crazed ex-boyfriend copycats The Zombie," I said, thinking of what the newspaper headline might be.

"You think I did it?" Jim said.

"Stranger things have happened."

"If I did it, why would I be helping Robbie right now? Why wouldn't I just let him take the rap?"

"Interesting point," I said.

"You got a lot of nerve, Mr. Colt. I'm appalled that you would even suggest something so ridiculous. Like I told you, I loved Alison. I'm just as upset as everyone else about this shit."

Maybe, I thought. Maybe Jim Ballard was just as upset as everyone else. Or maybe he was just a good actor. A con man. Maybe he was trying to hide something. Or maybe, in his own alcohol-soaked mind, he was telling the truth. Maybe he killed Alison and didn't even remember it. A jumble of possibilities bobbled through my brain like Ping-Pong balls in a lottery cage.

Jim made a series of turns, and then slowed and braked to a stop.

"Get out," he said.

"Can I take the blindfold off?"

"No. Leave it on."

I climbed out of the car and stood there until Jim came around. We were close to the ocean. I could hear it. I could smell it.

"Now what?" I said.

"Put your left hand on my shoulder."

I put my left hand on his shoulder. He started walking, and I followed. He told me to watch my step. We went from sand to a boardwalk. Soon after that we stepped onto a swaying wooden platform, a floating dock of some sort. We walked a few more feet and then stopped. Jim guided my hand to a steel rail.

"We're getting on a boat?" I said.

"Yeah. Climb aboard."

I climbed aboard, and Jim guided me one way and then another. He finally directed me down a narrow stairway, what nautical types call a ladder. The sounds from the outside world, the squawking of the gulls and the whooshing of the waves and the rumble of a diesel engine in the distance, disappeared as Jim secured the hatch.

CHAPTER SIXTEEN

I asked again if I could take the blindfold off.

"Go ahead," Jim said.

I took it off. Jim was standing there pointing my own gun at me. He had the revolver in one hand and a bottle of tequila in the other. He'd already uncapped the liquor, and his lips were shiny from taking a drink of it.

"Where's Robbie?" I said.

"There are two drawers under the bed. Pull out the one on the right."

"Fuck you."

He aimed the .38 at my head, cocked the hammer back. "I think you better do what I tell you to do. I don't want to make a mess on my boat, but I will if I have to."

I didn't think he was going to shoot me. Plenty of people had seen us leaving Jake's Key West Saloon together. If I went missing, Jim Ballard would be the prime suspect. I didn't think he was going to shoot me, but I wasn't quite willing to bet my life on it. I decided not to call his bluff just yet.

"All right," I said. "Easy with that thing. It has a sensitive trigger."

We were in a bedroom. It was a fairly large space for a boat, maybe the first mate's cabin or even the captain's quarters. There was an old wooden ship's wheel and two shaded lamps attached to the bulkhead behind the mattress. The lamps were on hinged arms that you could swivel out for reading or whatever. Heavily varnished teak and polished brass everywhere. A pair of drawers had been built into the pedestal beneath the bed, with coarse lengths of mooring line serving as pulls.

I knelt down and opened the drawer on the right. It was full of kinky sex equipment. There were whips and chains and slings and ball gags. There was a feather duster and a spanking paddle and some vibrators in an assortment of colors, shapes, and sizes.

There were some other things I couldn't readily identify. Metal clamps that looked like something from a hardware store.

"Get the handcuffs out," Jim said.

I got the handcuffs out. "These?"

"Not those, the leather ones."

I found the ones I figured he wanted. I held them up, and he nodded in approval.

"Get on the floor," he said. "Facedown, with your hands behind your back."

I did as instructed. A few seconds later, I felt the leather cuffs tighten around my wrists. I heard a chain being pulled from the drawer, and then felt it being wrapped around the lower part of my legs.

"Have you lost your fucking mind?" I said. "Do you know how many people saw us walk out of that bar together?"

He ignored me.

"Turn over," he said.

"What?"

"Turn over."

There's nothing scarier than a drunk guy who doesn't give a shit. A drunk guy with a gun. I turned over onto my back and immediately there was a towel pressed against my face. I smelled something medicinal for a few seconds, and then the world faded away.

When I woke up, I was in the water and the boat was rapidly chugging away from me. There was no land in sight. He had taken me way offshore and dumped me overboard.

The perfect murder.

Now I knew why he'd wanted the leather handcuffs instead of the steel ones. The steel ones might have left marks on my wrists. He'd taken the cuffs and chains off before dumping me into the water. If he'd left them on, it would have been obvious that I'd been murdered. Now, if my body washed ashore, there would be no signs of foul play. No bullet holes, no bruises, no cuts or scrapes or abrasions. No evidence that my limbs had been restrained. Good old Jim had taken me out on his yacht for a nice afternoon cruise, and I had fallen overboard. He'd tried to save me, but I had gone under and had never come back up.

Right now Jim was probably navigating to a location several miles away. From there he would wait until sunset, and then call the Coast Guard. By the time they initiated a search and rescue effort, it would be completely dark outside. They would never find me. Not that it mattered. By sunset I would probably be dead anyway.

I thought about dunking my head and taking that first breath. Maybe it would be better to die on my own terms than to struggle futilely and wait for the inevitable. I thought about it.

The fact that I was in tropical waters and in no danger of hypothermia gave me little comfort at the moment. I could only tread water for so long. My muscles would fatigue and cramp, and then I would sink and drown.

I looked at my watch. If I could only make it until tomorrow morning, I thought. If I could only stay afloat for about fifteen hours. Then I might stand a chance. The Coast Guard would be looking for me, and they might be able to find me after the sun came back up. It wasn't likely, but it was possible. I decided to at least try. As long as I was breathing, there was still hope.

I managed to get my shoes off, first one and then the other. Next I shrugged out of the black John Fogerty tour T-shirt. I left my pants on. I'd heard horror stories about men skinny-dipping in the ocean. I didn't want any fish coming up and nibbling on my junk. Plus, I still had my wallet and my car keys. If I survived, I would need them. If I didn't, at least I would be easy to identify.

I felt twenty pounds lighter without the shoes, and about twenty degrees cooler without the shirt. The late afternoon sun was a bitch. It was going to fry my back and shoulders, but I'd been sweating profusely with the black T-shirt on. Sunburn I could handle. Dehydration was another story.

"Help," I shouted, but I knew it was no use. In every direction there was only ocean and sky. The vastness of it was overwhelming. I'd never felt so lost and so alone.

I tried to relax and just float for a while, but the sea was choppy and the waves kept washing over my face. I tried to keep my breathing regular and think about happy things. I tried not to think about how much my arms and legs ached already.

For some reason the song "Spiritual" by the late great John Coltrane started playing in my head. It reminded me of the night I first met Juliet. It was at a club called Lyon's Den. It was a Tuesday night in April. I had gotten a call earlier in the day from an old friend who played bass guitar. He invited me to the club, said he'd make sure I was treated well by the bartenders. I went alone. The band played a variety of music, everything from Motown to modern rhythm and blues and jazz standards. They had a sax player, keyboards, drums, lead guitar, and bass. I had known Tyler, the bass player, since we were kids. He got me a seat in the front row. Halfway into the second set, I noticed this really cute brunette sitting with three other women at the table next to mine. She kept looking over at me, smiling, and stirring her drink with a swizzle stick. I figured she was out of my league. She was younger, for one thing, by about ten years, and she was beautiful. She had the kind of skin that looks tanned all year, and I could tell she had a nice body, even though she was sitting down. She wore a crisp white shirt with lace around the collar. One of her friends got up, walked to my table, and asked me if I'd like to dance. They were playing an old Meatloaf song called "Two Out of Three Ain't Bad." While we danced, she whispered that it was her girlfriend Juliet's birthday. She said Juliet wanted to meet me.

"Me?" I said, acting flattered but not really believing what I was hearing.

"She thinks you're hot."

After the Meatloaf song, I walked to their table and introduced myself. Juliet and I struck up a conversation about, of all things, Area 51. About the possibility that extraterrestrial aliens had landed on Earth and there was some sort of government cover-up about it. You can really get going on a subject like that after a few cocktails.

The band went into another slow song, "Spiritual" by saxophonist John Coltrane, the same song playing in my head now. I asked Juliet to dance, and I started falling in love with her the minute our bodies met on the floor. We made a date for the following Saturday, and the rest is history. Juliet and I have had our ups and downs through the years, but we've always managed to come out hand in hand.

I thought about her and how she had practically begged me not to take this job in Key West. As usual, she'd been right. I should have left it alone.

I looked at my watch. An hour had passed. If I could make it one hour, maybe I could make it two. That's how I had to think about it. In small increments. Maybe I could eat this elephant one bite at a time.

I wondered what the world record was for treading water in the open sea. Surely someone had done it for more than fifteen hours. Surely it was humanly possible. If that person could do it, I could do it. One second, one minute, one hour at a time.

I was psyching myself into thinking I might actually stand a chance when I saw the dorsal fin of something very large speeding directly toward me.

The John Coltrane song that had been playing in my head came to an abrupt stop.

It was replaced by the theme to *Jaws.*

CHAPTER SEVENTEEN

The big fin kept coming, and then I saw another. And another. There were a dozen or more. I was surrounded by them.

I might have been able to fend off a single shark. I've heard of it happening. I have a friend whose daughter was attacked while surfing the waters between St. Augustine and Daytona. She was out there alone when she saw the fierce predator swim by, and when it came back after her, she did the only thing she could think of: she punched it in the nose. It took a bite the size of a Chihuahua out of her fiberglass surfboard, and then swam away. My friend's daughter made it back to shore without a scratch.

So I might have been able to handle one shark.

But not a dozen.

If one of them bit me, the blood would attract the others, and a feeding frenzy would ensue. Now there was no hope. I was going to die. It was almost a certainty. As Buck Owens used to say: adios, farewell, good-bye, good luck, so long.

I was expecting to be torn apart limb by limb when a shiny gray snout emerged and started making a nasally staccato laughing sound.

Dolphins.

Fucking dolphins!

They all started laughing, and I started laughing right along with them. I laughed until it hurt. A sense of relief washed over me, a wave of euphoria like I'd never felt before. Now I knew what an eleventh-hour death-row pardon felt like.

The dolphins swam around playfully and jumped and splashed and nudged me with their slick bodies. They weren't going to eat me. They were going to help me. At least I hoped they were.

I latched onto one of the dorsal fins, and my amiable aquatic friend started towing me one way and then the other. Just playing around. I decided my dolphin was female. I decided to give her a name. Lucille. That was a good name for a dolphin. It was playtime for Lucille and the gang, but I figured eventually they would continue toward their destination. And a few minutes later they did. The school started swimming westward, toward the sun. I had no other point of reference, so I had no idea where we were going. From Key West, Jim Ballard could have taken me out to the Atlantic. In that case, we were headed toward Florida. If Jim had dumped me deeper into the Gulf, we were headed toward Mexico.

Mexico was a long way away. I would never make it to Mexico. I would weaken from dehydration and lose my grip on Lucille, and then I would sink and drown. But that didn't happen. I got lucky. About thirty minutes into our journey, I spotted an island straight ahead. The sun was getting low and blinding me and I could barely see it. It appeared to be tiny, probably not even a dot on the map, and there were no other land masses in sight. But it was a chance.

The dolphins started veering north.

"Lucille, this is where I get off," I said.

I let go of her fin and she swam on without looking back.

"Thank you," I said.

I started freestyling it toward the shore. When I got to within maybe a hundred yards, I saw someone paddling a kayak near the south side of the island. I kept swimming. It was a young boy. Maybe nine or ten. When he saw me splashing toward him, he pulled the kayak onto a dry finger of land and ran away shouting, *Daddy!* He seemed very alarmed, which was understandable. It's not every day you see a wild-eyed pink-skinned monster with long hair and a beard wash in with the seaweed.

I crawled from the water onto the bank and lay there staring at the sky and breathing heavily. It wasn't a nice comfortable sandy beach. It was rocky, and the rocks were digging into the skin on my back and shoulders. But it was land. Blessed land. I never thought I would feel it beneath me again.

A few minutes after I landed, a man wearing neon green swimming trunks and a matching pair of water shoes trotted over and said, "Are you OK?"

"I think so," I said. "Can you help me up?"

"Who are you?"

"My name's Nicholas Colt. Someone just tried to kill me."

He extended his hand and we locked wrists and I struggled to a standing position. My ears were clogged with seawater, my head reeling with vertigo.

"Think you can make it to the house?" the man said.

"How far is it?"

"Not far. Just past those trees."

"Where are we?" I said.

"It's a private island you can rent by the week. I'm here with my wife and our boys."

"You have a boat?"

"Yes. It's also a rental. We're from Canada, and—"

"I need to get back to Key West," I said.

"That's no problem. I can take you to Marathon. It's only a five-minute boat ride from here. From Marathon you can take a taxi down or rent a car or whatever."

He seemed anxious to help. He probably wanted me out of his hair as quickly as possible, so he and his family could get on with their vacation.

I still felt a little woozy. "Maybe I better rest for a few minutes," I said.

"Sure. Come on up to the house."

He led me to a boardwalk and then to the cottage. We walked inside. He introduced me to his wife, Vera, and their two sons. Justin was the one I'd seen in the kayak. The other boy was only six. His name was Aaron.

"And I don't think I caught your name," I said to the man.

He laughed. "Sorry about that. Ralph Parker."

We shook hands.

"Is there a phone here?" I said.

"In the kitchen."

I called Juliet, told her to ignore any future reports of my untimely demise. I figured the Coast Guard search would be all over the eleven o'clock news. I didn't go into a lot of detail. I told her it was just a big mix-up. I didn't want her to be worried. She said she would call Brittney and tell her right away.

She was surprisingly cool about the whole thing. Or maybe resigned was a better word. It seemed maybe she had given up on trying to talk me out of staying on this case. She didn't raise her voice or start crying or anything. Then again, she said she'd taken a Valium not long before I called.

After talking to Juliet, I walked back to the living room and sat with the Parker family for a while.

"Did you swim all the way here?" Aaron said.

"I had a little help," I said. "You wouldn't believe it if I told you."

"Yes I would. What happened?"

I told him about the dolphins. I told him about the one named Lucille.

"Wow," he said. "That's *cool*."

The boys prodded me for more adventure stories, but Ralph must have seen how weary I was getting. He interceded on my behalf.

"You guys run along and play now," he said to the boys.

Justin and Aaron grabbed a couple of flashlights and went outside. Vera fixed me a cup of tea, and Ralph gave me a shirt to put on and a pair of flip-flops. They seemed interested in my story, so I told them all about my little ill-fated ocean cruise. It gave them something unusual to take back to their friends in Canada. They were very nice people. I told them so, and I thanked them for their kindness.

"There's an extra room," Vera said. "You can stay here tonight."

"I wouldn't want to impose."

"We insist. Come on, I'll show you to your room. You look exhausted."

She was right. I barely had enough energy to stand on my own.

Ralph loaned me a pair of pajama bottoms and I climbed into the bed Vera led me to and slept for nearly twenty-four hours. I only got up to use the bathroom and to get drinks of water. Twice, Vera brought food to my room on a TV tray, and both times I sat up and ate and then went back to sleep.

Finally, almost a day later, I woke up and felt as though I'd gotten enough rest.

Someone had washed and dried and folded my pants and boxer shorts. They were on top of the dresser, along with a clean T-shirt. I walked out to see if it was OK to take a shower, but the house was empty, so I found a towel and helped myself. By the time I got cleaned up and dressed, Ralph had returned and was loading a twelve-pack of beer into the refrigerator. He said Vera and the boys were still out exploring.

"I'm feeling better," I said. "Maybe I should go now."

"Won't you stay for dinner?"

"I would like to, but I really need to get back."

"Ok. I'll just leave a note here for Vera."

Ralph and I walked to the dock and boarded the rental boat, and he ferried me over to Marathon. He asked me if I needed money for cab fare. I told him I was OK.

I climbed out of the boat. Every muscle in my body was sore from the swim yesterday.

"Thanks again," I said. "Next time you and your family come to Florida, give me a call. I'll take you to the best seafood restaurant on the East Coast."

"Angels were watching over you yesterday, Nicholas."

"I think you're right," I said.

"Take care, my friend."

I watched as he motored back toward the little island.

CHAPTER EIGHTEEN

I found an ATM and withdrew four hundred dollars. I figured it would cost me half that to get back to Key West. Two hundred bucks to go forty-eight miles.

The first two cabbies I approached said they didn't have time. The third said OK, and I climbed into a minivan that smelled like cheap cigars and dirty diapers. The driver was a guy named Charlie. I couldn't handle the smell, so I told him to take me to the nearest rental car place. I picked out a black Ford Focus. It had a built-in GPS system, which I thought might come in handy. The guy at the counter said I could drop it off at the office in Key West tomorrow. I said OK. I paid with my debit card, and an hour later I was back in my hotel room.

Luckily, I still had my wallet and my car keys. Missing in action were my cell phone and my .38. Not to mention a fairly new pair of Sperry Top-Siders and my T-shirt from the John Fogerty concert.

I spread all the wet things from my wallet out on the dresser. I still had the business card Detective Craig Sullivan had given me, and I was about to call him when my room phone rang. I answered.

"Hey, Nicholas. This is Wesley West again. I tried your cell phone, but it kept going to voice mail. We said eight, right?"

I looked at my watch. It was almost nine. "I've had a pretty rough couple of days, Wesley. I don't think I'm going to be able to make it."

"Sorry to hear that. I bought beer and a meat-and-cheese tray and some nice crackers. I was hoping we could make a night of it. But if you can't make it, you can't make it. By the way, some detective came by asking about you. I told him you'd been over here looking for me the day Alison Palmer was killed, just like you said."

I felt bad. Wesley had come through for me, and now I was standing him up.

"Give me an hour," I said. "I can't stay late, but I can come over for a little while."

"Cool. Yeah, just come on over whenever you're ready."

I hung up and tried to call Detective Sullivan. An answering machine picked up and told me to call 911 if this was an emergency. I dropped the receiver into the cradle, stripped, and took another hot shower. For some reason, the water on the island had left me feeling as though I was covered with some sort of film.

Sullivan still wasn't answering his phone when I got out. Maybe he was sitting somewhere with a tall, cool glass of *Fuck The World* in front of him. Even homicide detectives have to call it a day at some point. I thought about filing the report with someone else, decided against it. I could talk to Sullivan tomorrow. The fewer police detectives I got involved with, the better; and I was a little worried that the cops would believe Jim's version of the story, not mine. If they believed Jim, that I'd been drinking and went for a swim and didn't come back up, then I was the one who would be in trouble. Jim could produce a firearm registered in my name, a gun I'd had no business carrying. No telling what kind of story he might make up.

After considering the possible outcomes for a few minutes, I wondered if I should even talk to Sullivan tomorrow. It was something I needed to think about.

I called Juliet, told her I still wasn't dead. She gave me umpteen rations of hell this time. I told her to take another Valium.

I got dressed and drove over to Wesley's place. I hadn't brought a second pair of shoes to Key West with me, so I was wearing the flip-flops from Ralph Parker. I didn't like driving in them, and I felt naked without my cell phone and my gun.

I knocked and Wesley opened the door and I walked into his apartment.

"Nice place you have here," I said.

"Thanks. I do OK for a lounge singer, I guess."

There was a sectional sofa and a big television and a round coffee table with a snack tray and some magazines on it. There was a framed poster on the wall, a promo with a list of tour dates for a band called Freak Willy. Near the television there were two acoustic guitars on stands. One was a Martin, the other a Takamine. Both fine instruments.

"Choose your weapon," Wesley said.

I picked up the Martin, sat on the sofa, and strummed an open G chord. I hadn't held a guitar in a while. It felt strange, and my fingers started aching right away.

The high E string was a little out of tune. I tweaked it by ear.

"Nice ax," I said.

"Thanks. I have an electronic tuner if you want to try that."

"I think it's OK now. Your E was just a little sharp."

"Can I get you a beer?" he said.

"Do you have any coffee?"

"I can make some."

"That would be great."

He went to the kitchen and started a pot of coffee. When he came back, he grabbed the other guitar and sat across from me on a wooden stool.

He started strumming a twelve-bar blues progression. I played some lead notes over it, best I could with my crippled hand. I'd lost all my calluses, and after a few minutes my fingertips started getting sore.

"That sounds great," Wesley said. "Show me what you were doing there."

I played the notes slowly while he watched, and then again while he tried to play along. He was struggling with it. His hands looked as though they might have been more at home turning a wrench.

"It's just a scale," I said. "But you're going to have to practice these runs using all four fingers. It'll take some time, but you'll get the hang of it eventually."

"It's hard," he said. "I've always been mostly a rhythm player."

I pointed at the poster. "Did you play in that band?"

"Yeah, for a few years. We were based in Atlanta, played all up and down the East Coast. The lead guitar player never wanted to show me anything, though. It was like he guarded that shit. Like a magician with his tricks or something."

"I invented some of those riffs I just showed you," I said. "But they're really not that difficult once you learn a few scales and learn how to fingerpick a little."

"You're a good teacher, Nicholas. I appreciate it."

We played some more and I drank a few of cups of coffee and he drank a couple of beers. The coffee was extraordinary. Wesley said it was something called Kona, shipped all the way from Hawaii. He had a bottle of Jack Daniels that hadn't been opened yet, and I was tempted to let him crack the seal and pour me a big glass. But I knew alcohol would make me sleepy, and I had some late-night work to do. So I stuck with coffee. I ate some ham and cheese and celery sticks from the tray on the coffee table, along with some sort of meat pâté that you spread on fancy little crackers with a fancy little knife. It wasn't foie gras, but something like that. The salty crackers irritated the blisters on my fingertips. I tried wiping them with one of the burgundy cloth napkins folded elegantly there beside the tray of hors d'oeuvres, but it didn't help much.

"I need to be running along," I said. "My fingers feel like someone burned them with matches. But this was fun. Thanks for having me over."

"Any time, Nicholas. You should think about teaching guitar for a living. You're really good at it."

"Thanks," I said.

"You know what I always wanted to learn?"

"What's that?"

"The lead solo to that song y'all did called 'Dead Ringer.'"

It was one of Colt .45's biggest hits. The studio version was layered with overdubs, but I'd written a solo for the stage shows that sounded almost as good.

"Another night," I said. "That's a really complicated part. It's going to take some time to teach it to you."

"But you'll come over again sometime and show me?"

"Sure."

"You promise?"

I laughed. "I promise, Wes."

"You really should think about teaching professionally. No shit."

"I don't know. Maybe."

I was once considered one of the best guitarists in the world. I was one of the best, but I couldn't play at that level anymore because of my ruined hand. So fuck it. I didn't want anything to do with the guitar. And I sure as hell didn't want to sit around in some closet with carpet on the walls and show pimply-faced kids how to play Metallica on their Les Paul knockoffs. Wasn't going to happen.

"I'll be at the lounge again Sunday and Monday night," Wesley said. "If you're still there."

"I'll probably still be there. I'll come down and check you out. Hell, if I get drunk enough, I might even play one with you this time."

That wasn't going to happen either.

Before I stood up to go, I lifted Wesley's copy of *Guns Magazine* from the coffee table and started flipping through it. It was the latest edition, and I hadn't seen it yet.

"You like to shoot?" Wesley said.

"Sometimes."

"Check this out."

He walked to the bedroom and came back holding a Colt M1911 .45-caliber semiautomatic pistol. He handed it to me.

I looked it over. "A classic," I said. "Very nice."

"Vietnam era. I found it at a gun show in South Carolina."

"Want to sell it?"

He stared at the wall for a second, and then looked back at me. "You looking to buy a gun?"

"I'm always looking," I said. "I'll give you five hundred for it. Two now, and three more when I see you at the bar Sunday night."

"I'll take six," he said.

The gun wasn't worth six hundred, but I didn't feel like dickering. I needed a weapon. Someone had tried to kill me yesterday, and I didn't know why. And I had a criminal record, so it wasn't like I could just walk into a pawnshop and buy a piece anymore.

"Deal," I said. I pulled two hundred dollars out of my pocket and handed it to him. "I'll give you the rest Sunday."

"I have some other Vietnam memorabilia if you're interested," he said.

I was interested. Intrigued, at least. I still didn't know how the Jim Ballard situation was going to play out, and I didn't want to come up short on firepower if I ended up going head-to-head with him.

"Let's see what you have," I said.

CHAPTER NINETEEN

It was almost midnight when I left Wesley's apartment. I wondered if Jim Ballard was at the club, telling everyone about the horrible accident earlier, about me falling off his boat and drowning. I imagined it was on all the local news channels.

Which was fine with me. At some point during my visit with Wesley West, while I was watching those thick concrete fingers of his fumble through the lead runs I was showing him, it occurred to me that it might be best to roll over and play dead for a while. The Coast Guard probably wouldn't spend more than a couple of million dollars looking for me. They could send Jim Ballard the bill.

Wesley had shown me some souvenirs from a war we were both too young to have fought in, some of which weren't exactly legal. He had that stuff, and I was going to roll with being dead for a while. We had an understanding. Wesley said he would ignore the news reports of my little boating incident. My secret was safe with him, he said, as long as his secrets were safe with me.

I tried calling Juliet. She wasn't answering her phone, so I left her a message.

At 12:16 I drove by Jake's Key West Saloon. My GMC Jimmy was still parked where I'd left it. The police hadn't come to tow it away yet. I pulled in behind it, indiscreetly opened the driver's side door, grabbed my netbook and my camera bag. I shut the door and got back into the Focus and drove around for a while. Jake's Escalade was in the parking lot, as was the Porsche I'd seen earlier. 2FAST4U. Jim Ballard's Audi wasn't there. The rest of the cars were regular old heaps anyone might drive. I didn't figure any of them belonged to a wealthy guy like Jim. The band was playing, which meant they'd found a substitute for Robbie Asbury. From what I could hear, they sounded pretty good.

I didn't think anyone had seen me come or go at the hotel earlier. I decided to leave all my things there and check in at another place. That way everyone in Key West could go on thinking I was at the bottom of the ocean.

I withdrew some more cash. I bought a bottle of rum and a quart of grapefruit juice at a liquor store, and I bought some clothes and shoes and a cheap suitcase and some other things at Kmart. I checked into a dump called Reefer's Inn under the name Douglas Gibson. I told the lady at the counter that my friends call me Doug. She was speeding on something, and looked about as interested as a squirrel with a math book.

I went to my room and turned on the television. They were talking about the financial crisis in Europe, but it didn't take long for the news to cycle back to the story about me. According to Jim Ballard, I had been drinking heavily and had decided to go for a dip. Then I just disappeared. The Coast Guard was still looking for me, and would continue their efforts into tomorrow, the reporter said.

I kept hoping they would cut to a shot of Jim Ballard's yacht, and I hoped there would be a big sign somewhere showing the name of the marina. That's what I wanted to know. I wanted to know where to find the son of a bitch. But they never showed a sign, and they didn't say where the boat was docked.

I opened my netbook. I'd memorized the tag number to Jim's Audi, so I planned on using it to find his home address. I doubted he would be there, but it was worth a try.

Unfortunately, Reefer's Inn didn't have a Wi-Fi signal, so I mixed myself a rum and grapefruit juice and drank until I passed out.

CHAPTER TWENTY

The zombies have abandoned their motorcycles. They're on horses now, riding along the dusty road to Dodge at a slow pace. They're all dressed like cowboys, some with tie-dyed headbands and peace-sign necklaces and puffy-sleeved shirts, incongruously leftover from their previous hippie attire. One of them has a Spanish guitar slung over his shoulder. There's blood and chunks of flesh dripping from their chins, indicating they have dined recently.

"How much farther to Dodge?" Boomer says.

"A few more miles, I reckon," says Rex.

"You reckon? What kind of talk is that?"

"Everyone in the Old West talks like that, dumbfuck. When in Rome."

"We ain't nowhere near Rome, I can tell you that."

"Shut up, Boomer. Hey, guys, lookee yonder."

Rex points, and the camera pans to a small wooden cabin in the distance.

"Let's check it out," Grady says.

They gallop toward the house. When they get there, a woman wearing a long dress is standing on the porch with a double-barreled shotgun.

"Howdy, ma'am," Rex says.

The woman points the gun at him. "You boys ride along now," she says.

"Well that's not very hospitable," Rex says. "All we want is a drink of water, and some water for our horses."

"I said ride along!"

One of the zombies dismounts his horse and starts walking toward the woman. She aims the gun and fires and the unnamed goon's head explodes. He falls to the ground.

Rex cringes, wipes the spray of blood from his face and forehead with a red bandana. All the zombies start dismounting now. The woman only has one more shot left, and by the time she pulls the trigger, one of the zombies has already grabbed the barrel and directed it skyward. Rex knocks the woman to the ground, and the zombies descend on her like a flock of vultures. As the scene dissolves, you can hear them slurping and sucking and chewing…

At ten-thirty Thursday morning the maid pounded on the door and startled me out of my zombie nightmare. I got up and peeked out and told her to come back later. I was still sleepy. I'd only gotten about five hours. I thought about going back to bed, but I didn't.

The rum bottle was nearly empty, but there was still plenty of grapefruit juice. I uncapped it and took a big swig. It was warm and sour and felt like battery acid when it hit my stomach. I chased it with a cool glass of water from the sink.

I looked in the mirror. My eyes were almost as red as my nose. They were still sore and itchy from the saltwater, and I wished I'd bought some eye drops with my other supplies.

Along with some new duds, I'd purchased a set of hair clippers and some shaving gear and a pair of black-framed wayfarer reading glasses. I'd decided to cut off my hair and beard so nobody would recognize me. So nobody would come up to me and say, *Hey, I thought you were dead.* The disguise had worked for me once before, a few years ago when I infiltrated a white supremacist cult called the Chain of Light. I figured it would work for me again.

I sheared the hair on my face and head down to stubble. I thought about lathering up and shaving it all clean with the razor, but I finally decided to stick with jailhouse chic. I put the eyeglasses on. I looked like a cross between Bruce Willis and Clark Kent. I was a new man.

I checked out of the motel. I didn't want to stay in the same place more than one night while I was incognito. I figured I would be less likely to be identified if I kept moving. Anyway, Reefer's Inn sucked. The room was damp, and it smelled like stale potato chips.

I drove my rental car to the Key West office, told them I'd be needing it for a few more days. The guy at the counter tried to talk me into something bigger and more luxurious, but I liked the little Ford. It said, *Not a former licensed investigator illegally working on a murder case*, and that was the statement I wanted to make.

I went to McDonald's and bought a cup of coffee. I sat at a table in the back and used their Wi-Fi signal to get on the Internet. I did some research on Jim Ballard. I was able to find his home address and phone number through the DMV. Luckily, it was a real address and not a post office box. I only hoped it was current.

Jim had never been married. No bankruptcies. He'd been arrested several times, all misdemeanors. He'd bought a house a couple of years ago, and I saw that he had owned a BMW before the Audi. The BMW was an antique, a 1968 2800 CS. Several months ago the title on it had been transferred to a man named Drake Upton, who lived in Fort Lauderdale. It had sold for thirty-two thousand dollars.

I got an Egg McMuffin to go, and headed toward Jim Ballard's address. On the way, I stopped at the T-Mobile store and a bought a replacement for my cell phone. They let me keep the same number.

I thought about calling Detective Craig Sullivan and telling him that Jim Ballard had tried to kill me. That's what I had planned to do last night, but it would have been a mistake. Jim claimed my disappearance was an accident, and I had no way to prove otherwise. It was my word against his. I doubted Lucille the dolphin would be a very good witness. And while Jim was denying everything I said, he would undoubtedly spill the beans about my illicit investigative activities. When all was said and done, I would be the one going to jail. Not Jim Ballard.

So I needed to find something on Jim myself. I had a hunch he'd killed Alison Palmer. I had a hunch he'd killed her and made it look like the work of The Zombie. He could have anesthetized her, maybe with the same stuff he'd knocked me out with, and then he could have used a small circular saw to cut the top of her head off.

Step three: Reach in, scoop out brain.

Step four: Reattach skull with Krazy Glue…

It was a simple procedure, when you got down to it. It didn't require a lot of skill. Some of the analysts on CNN were speculating that The Zombie might be some kind of neurosurgeon, but I didn't think that was necessarily the case. You didn't need a lot of training to cut people open if you didn't want them to recover afterward.

Jim was the jealous ex-boyfriend. Insanely jealous, if what Darcy Clermont told me was true. He had a motive to kill Alison, whereas Robbie Asbury, to my knowledge, did not. I needed to find some evidence against Jim and then call it in anonymously. After that, I could show up alive and claim amnesia or something. That way Jim would be behind bars, and I would walk free. It was the only way the legal system was going to work for me, the only way for justice to be administered within the constraints of the law.

And if justice couldn't be administered within the constraints of the law, there was always plan B. Plan B involved procuring some of Wesley West's toys from the Vietnam War.

I cruised by Jim's house. His Audi wasn't in the driveway, but it might have been in the garage. Impossible to tell from the road. Jim lived in a nice neighborhood. Lots of two-story brick, lots of palm trees. Manicured lawns, privacy fences, expensive outdoor lighting fixtures.

I parked half a block away, in front of a property that was for sale. I called the number on the real estate sign, and the lady who answered said the house was currently vacant. She said it was in move-in condition, and that the owners were asking one-point-five.

Million.

Dollars.

She asked me if I would like to look at it. I told her yes.

I laid it on thick, made it sound as though I was very rich and very interested. I was neither, of course, but it gave me an excuse to park there on Jim's street for a while.

One and a half million dollars was a ton of dough, but it was less than Jim had paid for his place. Apparently the values had gone down over the past couple of years. I guessed they had gone down everywhere, even in ritzy neighborhoods like this.

I tried Jim's phone number, the one on record at the DMV. I didn't know if it was a landline or a cell, but whatever it was, it went to voice mail. I didn't leave a message. I didn't want him to know I was alive. I wanted it to be a surprise. If he had answered, I was going to block my number from his caller ID and pretend to be a telemarketer. I just wanted to know if he was home or not, and I figured I might be able to tell from the background noise. If there weren't any engines purring or glasses clinking or drunks jabbering, maybe he was at the house. But he didn't answer, so I still had no idea.

I sat there for a while and kept an eye on his front door. I was close enough to watch the place without making it obvious. At 1:24 someone pulled into the drive. It wasn't Jim. It was the Porsche I'd seen in Jake's parking lot. 2FAST4U. I tried to remember the name of the guy who owned it. Cale something or another. Meade. That was it. Cale Meade. He got out and walked to the entranceway and rang the bell. Stood there for a minute. Rang the bell again. Knocked. Looked at his watch and walked back to his car.

Before he drove away, I called the number I'd written on the back of Detective Sullivan's business card.

"Hello?" he said.

"It's me," I said.

I said it deep and flat, the way Jim Ballard talked.

"Jim?"

"Yeah."

"You buy a new phone or something?"

"I don't use the same one all the time," I said. "You know that."

"Where the hell are you, man? I'm at your house. You said to be here at one-thirty, and I'm here."

"I said one-thirty?"

Anyone who'd ever dealt with Jim Ballard knew that he was a drunkard prone to blackouts. I was counting on Cale buying into the total memory lapse, and he did.

"This shit's getting old, Jim."

"Sorry. To tell you the truth, I can't even remember why you were coming over."

"You're joking, right? You wanted me to get rid of that Beemer you sold a while back."

"Oh, yeah. That's right."

"So you still want me to do it, or what? Like I told you before, I'm going to need the cash up front."

"I still want you to do it," I said. "Just wait there at my house. I'll be there in a little while."

"How long?"

"Just wait there."

I hung up. It wasn't unusual for party boys like Jim Ballard to close down the after-hours clubs and then sleep until two or three in the afternoon. Maybe he'd driven up to Miami's South Beach last night. Maybe he'd tried to wash the murder of Nicholas Colt out of his system with alcohol. Maybe he'd tried to cleanse himself of that particular layer of filth. And if so, maybe he really had forgotten about the meeting with Cale. It was a distinct possibility.

I'd dealt with plenty of drunks over the years, as a musician and as a private investigator, and Jim Ballard was one of the worst I'd ever seen. The way he'd been tapping that bottle of Cuervo on his boat, it was a wonder he could even stand up. Much less remember scheduling a meeting.

So maybe he'd forgotten.

I was counting on it being something like that. Hoping it was, anyway. I was hoping Jim would show up eventually, sometime before Cale got tired of waiting. Before Cale started the Porsche and drove away.

Cale had mentioned getting rid of the Beemer. I assumed he meant the BMW Jim had sold to the guy up in Lauderdale. Apparently Jim wanted it to disappear for some reason, and apparently Cale with the 2FAST4U Porsche was in a position to drive up there and make it happen.

For a price.

There must have been something incriminating in that car, something Jim was determined to keep hidden.

I opened my netbook and lucked into finding an unsecured Wi-Fi signal. I looked up the BMW dealership in Fort Lauderdale, and then the number for the new owner of Jim's car. Drake Upton. I remembered seeing it before. What I didn't remember seeing was his age. Drake Upton was eighty-seven years old.

I called Lauderdale BMW first. It was the closest dealership to Drake's house, and I was hoping he took it there for service and maintenance. And, with a car that valuable, I was hoping an alarm system had been installed.

I got lucky on both counts. I talked to a guy named Phil in the service department. I pretended to be Drake Upton, and Phil gave me the information I needed.

I punched in Drake's number next. It rang five or six times, and he finally picked up. He sounded as though he might have recently swallowed a handful of gravel.

"Yeah?" he said.

"May I speak to Mr. Upton, please?"

"Speaking."

"This is Bill, at the service department over at Lauderdale BMW. How are you today, sir?"

"I already filled out your satisfaction survey," he said. "What do you want?"

"I know you did, Mr. Upton, and we appreciate your business, sir. What I wanted to talk to you about is the recall on your antitheft system."

"There's a recall?"

"I'm afraid so. You'll be getting a notice in the mail soon, and of course your new alarm system will be installed at absolutely no cost to you. In the meantime, we're offering to come to your house and adjust the sensitivity on your current system."

"You want to come to my house?"

"Yes. The service team here is determined to rectify this problem with as little inconvenience to the customer as possible. And of course the house call will also be free of charge."

"What's the problem with the alarm system?"

"Some of them have a faulty computer chip," I said. "Particularly on your model. And there have been several cars stolen recently in and around the Fort Lauderdale area. We just want to help you protect your property best you can until the recall parts come in."

"Well, I appreciate that," Drake said. "But the car's in the garage most of the time anyway. My eyesight's not so great anymore, you know, and—"

"That's fine," I said. "And I'm assuming there's a burglar alarm wired to your garage."

"Well, no, I never really saw any need for one."

"I see. Well, that tells me your car is more vulnerable to theft than what we're comfortable with. Would it be OK for me to drop by this evening and adjust your system for you? It won't take long."

"I guess that'll be all right. What time?"

"Is seven OK?"

"OK."

We said good-bye and disconnected.

CHAPTER TWENTY-ONE

I checked the distance from Key West to Fort Lauderdale on my computer. 189 miles. I figured I could make it in three hours, and then it would probably take me another thirty minutes to find Drake Upton's house. So I needed to leave Key West no later than three-thirty. That gave me a little over an hour and a half to wait and see if Jim came home. If Jim came home, money would change hands and the deal would be on.

One more feather in my cap when I made the anonymous call to the police.

I wanted that feather, but I also wanted to get to the BMW before Cale Meade got to it. I wanted to look it over, try to see why Jim wanted it back so badly. Try to see what he was so worried about. If Cale Meade got to it first, it would probably end up flattened by a crusher and stacked with a bunch of other similarly fated cars in a scrapyard somewhere. The steel would be shredded and sold as raw stock to a Chinese refrigerator factory or something, and whatever Jim was trying to hide would be gone forever. I wanted to get to it before that happened.

I thought about calling Drake Upton back and changing our appointment to an earlier time and leaving for Fort Lauderdale now. That way I would be sure to get to the car before Cale Meade did. I thought about it, decided against it. Cale wouldn't do the job today. Today would be for collecting the money, and for talking out a plan. Professional thieves don't just wander in on short notice and start grabbing things. Professional thieves thoroughly analyze the situation and make detailed plans. All that takes time. Cale was a professional. He wouldn't do the job today. I stopped worrying about it.

I killed a little time by calling a music store in Jacksonville and asking how much they charged for guitar lessons. Just out of curiosity. The cost was astonishing. Apparently you could make some decent money teaching an instrument. Not that I would ever seriously consider doing it for a living.

Another fifteen minutes went by. The Porsche was still parked in Jim's driveway, and Jim still wasn't home. Cale's windows were up, so I assumed the car was running. I figured he was keeping the air conditioner on, trying to stay cool and comfy while he waited. Probably not terribly concerned about his carbon footprint.

Instead of just twiddling my thumbs, I decided to do a little research on The Zombie. I didn't think Jim Ballard was the serial killer; but, if my hunch about his killing Alison was correct, then Jim had studied enough about The Zombie to do a respectable job of copying him, and a good detective always tries to get inside the mind of his suspect. Most of the time it doesn't help, but it never hurts. I wanted to know at least as much as Jim knew.

The information was sketchy, but twelve murders had been attributed to The Zombie so far, the most recent being Alison Palmer. Hers was the fourth in Key West. The other three Key West slayings were also women, and all of them had been between the ages of twenty-four and thirty-five at the time of their deaths. The eight remaining murders had occurred in eight different locations, all in southern states along the East Coast.

The first victim had been found nearly six years ago, in an abandoned warehouse near Greenville, South Carolina. Her name was Rebecca Groyo, and she was twenty-six years old.

The second was a thirty-one-year-old convenience-store clerk named Shelby Wilcox in Savannah, Georgia, found dead and brainless in the store's walk-in refrigerator.

The Zombie's third victim was the first man of the bunch, a retired high-school science teacher in Durham, North Carolina. His name was Lou Robinson. He was found dead in a La-Z-Boy recliner, with ten empty beer bottles on the table beside him. I wondered if the police had interviewed any of his former students as potential suspects. There must have been thousands of them.

The next murder was also in North Carolina, this one in Wilmington. A twenty-nine-year-old army captain had been home on leave, and had been out drinking with some friends. They found her car at one of the local taverns, and they found her body in the woods.

The next victim, the fifth, was the one farthest north. It happened in Lynchburg, Virginia. An obstetrician named Kari Elm had been called to the hospital at three o'clock in the morning to deliver a baby. The mother and the newborn made it. Kari Elm didn't.

The sixth murder occurred in Key West, but then The Zombie went back north to Brunswick, Georgia for the seventh. The body was found in a creek bed under a railroad bridge. The victim actually lived and worked in St. Augustine, Florida. It was the second male of the group, a registered nurse named Roger Englehart.

The eighth slaying occurred in the seaside community of Jupiter, Florida. A thirty-three-year-old accountant from Cocoa Beach had checked into the Holiday Inn for a tax seminar. One of the maids found her resting peacefully in bed the next afternoon. A little too peacefully.

The ninth murder, the last of the eight that hadn't occurred in Key West, was particularly gruesome. It happened in Cape Fear, North Carolina. The victim, a twenty-eight-year-old bank teller who moonlighted as a bartender on the weekends, had a flat tire on her way to work one morning. They found her in a ditch near the overpass where her car broke down. Not only was her brain missing, her tongue had been cut out and all her teeth had been pulled.

The four murders in Key West were spread out over three years. The one before Alison's, the one I heard about on the radio on my way to see John Fogerty at the St. Augustine Amphitheatre, had also been augmented by additional mutilations. In that one they had found the woman's heart where her brain should have been.

At 3:03 Cale Meade backed out of Jim's driveway, drove to the end of the street, and took a right at the stop sign. I decided to follow him. I didn't know if he had given up on Jim coming home, or if he had talked to Jim on the phone and arranged to meet elsewhere. I wasn't very worried about him mentioning the earlier phone call from me. He had no reason to be suspicious. He was just a thief looking to make a buck, and moving forward with the job would be first on his mind.

And if he did mention the call, that would be OK too. It might plant a seed of fear in Jim's alcohol-soaked brain, and a fearful man tends to make irrational decisions and stupid mistakes. A little fear in Jim's heart might actually work to my advantage.

On my way to the intersection, a blue SUV with a Watson Realty sign passed me on the other side of the road. I guessed it was the agent I'd talked to on the phone, coming to show me the house. I felt bad about wasting her time, but not bad enough to turn around.

I followed Cale for ten minutes, and finally he pulled to the curb and parked at a meter and walked into a coffee joint called Perk-U-Now. I found a spot across the street where I could watch the shop. I didn't see Jim's Audi anywhere. A few minutes later, Cale walked out with a woman. It was the same woman who had dropped him off at Jake's Key West Saloon yesterday. Same white visor, same big sunglasses. Cale and his companion climbed into the Porsche and drove away. I followed them to a motel. It was playtime. I figured one or the other of them must have been married. Maybe both of them were.

I didn't care about any of that. All I cared about was that Cale had given up on meeting with Jim. At least for the time being. So that was that. I drove past the motel, made a U-turn at the next light, and headed for Fort Lauderdale.

CHAPTER TWENTY-TWO

I stopped at a Kmart in Miami and bought some khaki work clothes, a pair of sturdy black shoes with rubber soles, and a can of motor oil. I changed in the restroom, scuffed the shoes in the parking lot, worked a little of the motor oil and some grit from the pavement together in my hands, and wiped it on my new shirt and pants. I capped the oil, tied it into the plastic bag I'd carried it out in, and put it in the trunk along with the clothes I'd been wearing before I changed.

Tools. I needed tools.

I went back in and bought a set of jeweler's screwdrivers. They came in a little plastic case that fit in my shirt pocket. While I was at it, I bought a prepaid cell phone and a roll of duct tape. I used to own some fairly sophisticated surveillance equipment, but I ended up selling it during my love affair with heroin. I pawned it all and bought dope with the money. I thought the prepaid phone might come in handy as a poor man's audio bug.

I wanted to look as though I'd been working in the service department at Lauderdale BMW all day. The only thing missing from my costume was a patch on the shirt that said *BILL*, but I was counting on eighty-seven-year-old Drake Upton with bad eyes not noticing.

I got to his house at 7:07. It was dark already, but Drake's place had plenty of exterior lighting. He came walking out of the front door as I pulled into the driveway. He must have been watching for me. He was short and thin and bald, and he wore Bermuda shorts and a loud polyester shirt and leather sandals. Thick bifocals. He seemed to get around pretty well. No cane, no walker.

We met on the sidewalk in front of his house.

"Drake Upton," he said.

"Bill Johnson," I said. "Pleased to meet you."

We shook hands.

"You new at the shop? I don't think I've ever seen you there before."

"I've been there almost a year," I said. "Just part-time, though. I'm sure you know Phil, right?"

He nodded. "Well, you want to take a look at the car?"

"Sure. Is it in the garage?"

"Yeah. You got tools?"

I pulled the little plastic case out of my shirt pocket. "This is all I'll need today," I said.

"Can I see that?"

"Sure."

I handed him the case. I didn't know anything about the alarm system on Drake's BMW, or any other kind of alarm system for that matter, but the jeweler's screwdrivers looked like something a technician might adjust one with. Drake examined the box, handed it back.

"Come on in the house," he said. "We can get to the garage from in there."

Apparently Drake didn't know anything about car alarms either. I followed him inside.

We walked through the living room and into the kitchen. There was a breakfast nook with a bistro table and two stools next to a door that opened into the garage. Drake opened the door and motioned for me to enter.

"Watch your step," he said.

The garage floor was about eight inches lower than the rest of the house. It was covered with black-and-white vinyl tiles arranged in the pattern of a checkerboard. It reminded me of the tables at Kenny's Organic Grocery. Metal signs and advertising displays and other memorabilia from filling stations and tire stores adorned the walls. There was a yellowed Texaco calendar opened to June 1962, back when you could trust your car to the man who wore the star.

"Where did you get all this stuff?" I said.

"Petroliana, they call it. Kind of a hobby, I guess. I was quite the collector back in the day."

I pointed to a set of shelves lined with oil cans, dozens of them, each one a different brand.

"Are all those full?" I said.

"They're empty. Just for decoration."

I wondered if he might like the plastic Pennzoil container I'd bought at Kmart. I didn't ask.

"She's a beauty," I said, gesturing toward the shiny little BMW coupe. It was white with a medium-blue interior. All stock, all original, right down to the hubcaps.

"Thanks," Drake said. "Maybe we'll take it for a spin when you get done."

"Are the keys in it?"

He reached into his pocket. "Here you go."

He handed me a ring with at least twenty jingling hunks of metal on it. All shapes and sizes. I thought about asking him if he was also a janitor back in the day.

"I'll just be a few minutes," I said.

I wanted him to leave. I wanted to plant the audio bug, and I didn't want him to stand there watching me while I combed the car for evidence. He must have read my mind. He didn't *stand* there watching me. He pulled up a stool so he could be more comfortable.

I opened the driver's side door, found the lever and popped the hood, all the while checking for anything that looked unusual. So far there was nothing.

Drake had left the door leading from the garage to the house open, but it wasn't helping cool the garage much. It was hot and stuffy out there, the air heavy with the smells of baked floor tiles and tire rubber.

Sweat trickled down my back as I leaned into the engine compartment and pretended to tweak something with one of the screwdrivers. The motor was clean. The valve cover looked as though someone might have scrubbed it with a toothbrush. No corrosion on the battery terminals, no grease on the spark plug wires. Nothing. The whole thing was immaculate. Like it was built yesterday. I fiddled in there for a few minutes, and then opened the passenger's side door.

"Do you have a flashlight I can borrow?" I said.

"Sure."

He got up and walked into the house. While he was gone, I took a quick look under the seats and floor mats, front and back. I didn't find anything, not even a stray dust particle. Everything had been swept and vacuumed and polished and waxed. Everything looked showroom new.

"Here you go," Drake said.

He handed me the flashlight, sat back down on his stool.

I pulled a different screwdriver out of the plastic case, knelt on the garage floor and looked under the dash. I reached in with my tool and adjusted an invisible potentiometer.

"I think that should do the trick," I said. "It might be a little more sensitive than you're used to, but you won't have to deal with it for long. The recall parts should be in by next week."

The phone in the house rang. It sounded like the bell at a firehouse.

"I better get that," Drake said, moving toward the door. "It might be my grandson."

When he was out of sight, I walked around and opened the trunk. It was fairly large, and at first glance it appeared to be as clean as the rest of the car. I shined the flashlight into all the little recesses and crevices, and I was about to give up when something caught my eye. There was a tiny dark spot where the covering for the left rear wheel well met the trunk floor. I pressed the seam with my fingers, saw that the spot went deeper. I scraped it lightly with the blade of my screwdriver. It might have been something else, but it looked and acted like dried blood. I tapped some of the flakes from the tip of the screwdriver into the plastic case. I slid the tool into its slot, snapped the case shut and put it back in my shirt pocket. If it was blood, and if it was evidence from a crime, I had at least secured enough for a lab to perform a DNA test. The car, and any evidence it might contain, wouldn't exist for long once Cale Meade got his hands on it.

I closed the trunk and the hood and the doors, and walked into the house. It was at least twenty degrees cooler in there. I could breathe again. Drake was just hanging up the phone.

The phone. Damn it. I'd forgotten to plant the prepaid cell phone.

"It wasn't my grandson after all," he said. "It was some guy interested in buying the car."

"I didn't know it was for sale," I said.

"It's not, but with a classic car like that people make offers all the time anyway. I usually just tell them I'm not interested."

"Is that what you told them this time?"

"Actually, no. I've been thinking lately about getting a smaller place. I don't need all this room, and it's just so much to take care of. And the car, well, like I said, I don't drive much anymore, because of my eyesight. I really never should have bought it in the first place. So maybe it's time to let it go. If I can get a good price, of course."

"So is the person you talked to going to come and look at it?"

"Yeah, in about an hour. You're all done with the alarm?"

I thought about telling him I had one more thing to check out. I wanted to plant the bug, but I doubted he was going to leave me alone long enough. And I didn't want to press my luck by sticking around much longer. It would only take one phone call to expose me as a fraud.

"I'm done," I said.

"Good. It was a pleasure to meet you, Mr. Johnson."

"Likewise," I said.

We shook hands again. He was obviously trying to get rid of me. He didn't want a mechanic hanging around while he was trying to sell the car. It might have given the impression that the vehicle had problems.

Drake escorted me to the front door, and we said good-bye.

I drove out to the main drag, parked in front of a paint store with a *FOR LEASE* sign in the window. Another casualty of the weak economy, I thought. When given a choice, most people would rather eat than change colors. Priorities.

I climbed out of the Ford Focus and started walking. I could have kicked myself for not planting the audio bug. Now I was going to have to monitor Drake's place in person.

I left the .45 I'd bought from Wesley West in the glove compartment. I wanted to carry it, but I didn't want the trouble it would generate if a cop saw me lurking around Drake Upton's neighborhood. I'd lost my concealed weapons permit along with my PI license, and I didn't have any kind of paper on the .45. It was jail time waiting to happen.

I wanted to see who had called about buying the car. Maybe Jim Ballard had decided to go about it that way, rather than hiring Cale Meade to steal it for him. Or, maybe it was Cale, pretending to be a buyer but really just coming over to check out the security situation.

Or, maybe the buyer was someone else, someone totally unrelated to the case I was working on.

Maybe, but I didn't think so. It would have been too much of a coincidence. The caller had to have been Jim, or someone working for him. I knew for a fact Jim wanted to make the car disappear, and I had a hunch the blood flakes I'd dislodged in the trunk would end up revealing the reason why.

I casually strolled down the sidewalk, looking for a place to hide and wait. Across the street and a few houses down from Drake's place there was a house that looked to have been abandoned. Weeds in the yard, overgrown shrubs, foreclosure notice tacked to the front door.

I sat on the ground behind some bushes. It was perfect. I could clearly see Drake's driveway, but nobody could see me. It was almost eight-thirty, and the guy interested in the car was supposed to show around nine. If it turned out to be Jim Ballard, or Cale Meade, I planned to make an anonymous call to the police and let them handle it from there. If it turned out to be someone else, I planned to follow him and see where it led. If it didn't lead anywhere, I planned on spending a couple of days watching Pamela Wade, Phineas Carter's widow. I still had her Fort Lauderdale address in my computer.

I wanted to check her out, just to cover all the bases, but the deeper I got into this thing the more I doubted she—or the drug dealers she might have been keeping company with—had anything to do with Phin's death.

Phin and Alison had been murdered in the same apartment. There had to be a connection. I hadn't figured it out yet, but there had to be one.

I sat there in the weeds and waited and sweated and itched. The mosquitoes were tearing me up. They were huge. Big tropical motherfuckers. I made a mental note to bring a can of OFF! next time. Or a flamethrower. I hoped I wasn't going to need a transfusion before all was said and done.

At exactly nine o'clock a car pulled into Drake's driveway. It wasn't Jim Ballard, and it wasn't Cale Meade, and it wasn't someone totally unrelated to the case I was working on.

It was Robbie Asbury.

CHAPTER TWENTY-THREE

A voice behind me said, "What the hell you doing, mister?"

I turned and saw the vague outline of a man, standing there in the doorway of the house I thought to have been abandoned. There wasn't enough light to tell much about him. He was thin and shirtless. White baseball cap. That was about all I could see.

"Just resting my bones," I said.

"This here's my place, and I don't allow no trespassing."

I figured him to be a squatter. Eventually the law would come and run him off, but in the meantime he could stay out of the rain and have a nice comfortable place to drink or smoke crack or fuck. Whatever he was into. And when someone finally did tell him to move along, he would just take up residence in another place that had been slated for demolition or foreclosure. Free rent for life.

"Sorry," I said. "I was just leaving."

I rose to a standing position. I needed to get back to my car. I needed to do it quickly, before Robbie Asbury came and went. I needed to follow him and see what he was up to.

Robbie wasn't driving the Ford Ranger I'd seen him in before. He was running from the law, so it made sense that he'd changed vehicles. What didn't make sense was the one he'd changed to.

It was a neon-red Chevy Caprice, all tricked out with a lift kit and twenty-eight-inch wheels. It was about as inconspicuous as a firecracker. But maybe that was his strategy. Hiding in plain sight. Anonymity via extravagance. No cop in the world would expect a fugitive to be driving such a monstrosity.

"You hold on there," the squatter said. "I want to know what you were doing out here. You planning on robbing one of these houses around here or something? You planning on stealing a car?"

"If I was, you think I would tell you?" I said.

He put his hands on his hips. "Now what kind of a smart-ass answer is that?"

He was definitely high on something. He was starting to get loud, and I didn't need the attention. I was trying to be sneaky, and this idiot was cramping my style in a big way.

I walked to the stoop where he was standing.

"Look," I whispered. "I'm not a burglar or a car thief. I'm a private investigator, and you're making it hard for me to do my job."

"A real private investigator?" he said.

We were both whispering now.

"A real private investigator," I said.

"No shit? Just like that Magnum guy on TV, huh?"

"Yeah, just like him. Except I'm better looking."

He laughed, lit a cigarette. "Hey, don't most private investigators have a sidekick? You know, a guy who helps out from time to time? Maybe I could be your sidekick."

He reeked of tobacco and alcohol, and something I couldn't quite put my finger on. Something sweet. Crystal meth maybe. He was fucked-up, but maybe he could be of some use to me.

"You want to help me?" I said.

"Sure, man. What do you want me to do?"

I handed him a twenty-dollar bill. "See that bright red car over there with the big tires?" I said.

"Yeah, I see it. You could see that fucker from outer space."

"I want you to keep an eye on it for a few minutes while I go get my car. If a guy comes out and gets in it and starts to leave, I want you to walk over there and stall him for a while."

"That's it?"

"That's it. I'll be around in a black Ford Focus. I'll park it here in front of your house. Once you see my car, you can let the Caprice go."

"Man, this is exciting. Just like the movies or something."

"Don't forget. If a guy comes out and starts to leave, stall him."

"Got it," he said. "Hey, chief, what's your name anyway?"

I had no intention of giving this clown any of my personal information.

"Clete Purcel," I said, borrowing the name from a James Lee Burke novel I read one time. I was counting on him not getting the reference.

"I'll stay right here and watch, Mr. Purcel. You can count on me."

"You can call me Clete," I said. "Thanks. I won't be long."

"All right, Clete. You take care of yourself, buddy."

We were buddies now.

I turned and started strolling down the sidewalk, toward the main thoroughfare. I half expected the squatter to shout something at me from half a block away, but he didn't.

It took me about ten minutes to get to my car, and about two more minutes to drive back to the abandoned house. The Caprice was in the street now, and the squatter was standing at the driver's side door. He was leaning into the window and saying something. He'd come through for me. He was a good sidekick. That's what I thought until he turned and pointed back at my car.

"That's him," he said.

The Caprice started reversing slowly. The squatter just stood there with his arms folded across his chest and watched. He'd double-crossed me. The son of a bitch. My cover was blown, but not really. The bum had told Robbie I was a PI named Clete Purcel. Robbie had only seen me once, and I'd shaved my hair and beard since then. Maybe this was going to work out after all. I'd been wanting to talk with Robbie Asbury, and now I would finally get a chance. Anonymously.

Robbie kept reversing until the passenger's side window of his Chevy lined up with the driver's side window of my Ford. Robbie rolled his window down. I rolled my window down. Robbie aimed a pistol at my face and fired twice.

CHAPTER TWENTY-FOUR

When I saw what was coming, I pulled the lever on my bucket seat and dropped to a fully reclined position. Both bullets whistled over me and crashed through my passenger's side window. The Caprice screeched away in a cloud of smoke.

Two shots had been fired, and there were two holes. Fortunately, neither of them was in me. I felt myself to make sure. Sometimes you can be shot and not even know it. You can bleed to death before it even starts hurting. But I was OK. I hadn't been hit.

I straightened my seat, put the car in gear, and took off after the Caprice. My palms were sweaty and my mouth was dry and I felt a little shaky all over. I was rattled, and I was pissed. I wanted to stop and beat the shit out of the squatter, but I didn't have time. I reached over and pulled the .45 I'd bought from Wesley West out of the glove compartment, set it on the passenger's seat.

I didn't want to get into a gunfight with Robbie Asbury. That was the last thing I wanted. A gunfight would be a no-win situation for me. I would either be injured or killed, or I would injure or kill him. If I injured or killed him, I would go to prison. It wouldn't matter that it was self-defense. I was on probation and had no business carrying a deadly weapon. The DA would throw the book at me.

A gunfight was the last thing I wanted, but I would do whatever it took to protect myself. Jail is better than dead. Or so they say.

Robbie weaved his way through the neighborhood, turning left, right, left, right. The Caprice had more horsepower than my little Ford Focus, but it didn't handle well. Not with those humongous wheels. It didn't corner well, and it was top-heavy. So I was able to stay right on Robbie's tail for a while, even though he had the faster car. I dogged him like a shadow until he hung a left and headed down a long straightaway. Toward Sunrise Boulevard, where I'd parked at the out-of-business paint store. The gap between us widened. I floored the gas pedal, but I couldn't keep up. I was doing ninety, so he must have been doing a hundred or more. He wasn't even slowing down at the stop signs. Just barreling on through.

When he got to Sunrise, he took a right. He was going for the interstate. If he made it to I-95, that would be it. He would be able to shake me easily.

I screeched up to the blinking red light at the intersection, waited for a couple of cars to pass, and then followed. I was probably a quarter mile behind, but I could still see the garish custom taillights on the jacked-up Caprice. I worked my way over to the far left lane, traffic just heavy enough to be annoying.

Robbie ran the red light at the on-ramp to 95 north. It was a sharp curve on a steep incline, and he took it too fast. The Caprice rolled. I watched it tumble down the embankment, finally landing on its roof and spinning to a stop.

There were three or four cars in front of me at the turning light to the on-ramp. I pulled to the shoulder, jammed my pistol back into the glove compartment, cut the engine, and took off running toward the upside-down Caprice. I was first at the scene. I got on my hands and knees and peered through the crushed driver's side window, expecting to see a very banged-up corpse.

But Robbie was still alive.

"I can't feel my fucking legs," he said.

"Take it easy. You're going to be all right."

The air bags had deployed, and he'd been wearing his seat belt. No visible signs of injury. No blood, no bones poking through skin.

"Get me out of here," he said.

A guy and his girlfriend came running up from behind.

"Can we do anything?" the guy said.

"Call nine-one-one," I said. I turned back to Robbie. "Help is on the way. I don't want to move you, in case you have a spinal cord injury."

"I'm next," he said. His voice was hoarse. Raspy and weak. I got on my belly and moved in closer.

"What are you talking about?" I said.

"Jim Ballard is dead. I'm next."

His eyes closed and his jaw went slack. I felt his neck for a pulse. He was still alive. I shouted his name, but he wouldn't wake up.

I heard sirens in the distance, and a couple of minutes later an ambulance and a fire truck and two police cruisers showed up. One of the cops interviewed me about the accident, and then I walked back to the Ford Focus and hightailed it out of there. They were working on cutting Robbie out of the Caprice when I left.

CHAPTER TWENTY-FIVE

Marshal Mack Chillin is standing on the deck in front of his office when the zombies ride into town. Their horses clomp along the dusty street as though sandbags are tied to their legs. The zombies finally dismount and lead the exhausted animals to a water trough.

Mack is leaning on a post with his left hand, and his right hand is resting on the butt of his holstered revolver. He shouts across the way:

"You boys go ahead and water your horses, and then I want you to move along."

Rex turns and looks toward the marshal. "We've been riding for a long time," he says. "So we ain't gonna move along just yet. We're gonna walk in here to the Short Twig Saloon and have ourselves a beer. That's what we're gonna do. If anyone wants to find us, that's where we'll be."

Mack folds his arms across his chest and stands there rigidly while the zombies saunter single file through the swinging saloon doors.

Jeb, the messenger who told Mack that the zombies were coming, runs up to where Mack is standing now. He takes his dusty old raggedy hat off.

"Marshal Chillin, I tried to round up some men like you said. I tried, but soon as I told them about what was going on, they all got real quiet like. They got up from their seats, one by one, and walked away.

Didn't say a word, none of them. This town ain't nothing but a bunch of cowards, Marshal."

"At least I can count on you, Jeb. Come on in the office, and I'll deputize you."

Jeb hangs his head. "Gosh, Marshal, I got a wife and a kid at home to think about. I'd really like to help you. I really would."

"It's OK, Jeb. I understand. You ride on back to your farm now. Tend to your woman and your young'un. I'll be all right here."

Jeb nods. He puts his hat back on, turns and quietly walks away.

I parked a few blocks away at a Burger King. I switched on the radio, tuned it to an all-news station. Robbie had been telling the truth. Jim Ballard was dead. Another victim of The Zombie, according to the news story. They'd found him in his boat near the marina. Down in the galley, lying on the deck. Brainless. Apparently The Zombie had cut the lines and set the craft adrift. Two murders in as many days. The son of a bitch was getting bolder and bolder.

First Alison, and now Jim. Robbie said he was next. Why did he think that? Why would The Zombie systematically eliminate the three of them? Were Jim, Robbie, and Alison somehow connected to the serial killer? It didn't add up. Nothing was making sense at the moment. And what about Phineas Carter? What part, if any, did his murder play in all this?

Since I was in Fort Lauderdale already, I decided to drive by Pamela Wade's place. I doubted it would lead to anything, but I really didn't know where else to turn. I was baffled. Stumped. I found her address in my computer, used the GPS to point me in the right direction. I didn't have the energy to pull an all-night stakeout, but I figured I could watch her house for a while and see what happened. If nothing else, it would give me some time to think.

I made a couple of turns, and it didn't take long for me to realize I was heading into a bad part of town. There were several two-story concrete-block apartment complexes, their landscapes neglected and their faded pink-and-turquoise facades heavily marked with graffiti. Laundry drying on the balcony railings. Plastic kiddie toys abandoned in the dirt. There were basketball hoops with no nets, and swing sets with no swings. There were businesses with security bars over the doors and windows, and foreclosed homes boarded up with plywood. It was depressing as hell. It wasn't the kind of neighborhood you wanted to get lost in at night. Or any time of the day, for that matter.

Pamela Wade lived on one of the nicer streets. Apparently the residents were actually making an effort toward improvement. The yards were tidy, and some of the houses looked as though they'd recently been given a fresh coat of paint. I drove past Pamela's, turned around, pulled to the curb across the street.

It was almost eleven o'clock, and everything was quiet. I'd forgotten what day it was. I had to think about it for a minute. Thursday. It had been a long day. I let my seat back and sat there and rested for a while and watched the house. I didn't expect anything to happen, and nothing did. I sat there for over an hour, just trying to stay awake.

Stakeouts are the most boring part of being a private investigator, even a bogus one with no credentials. Stakeouts and paperwork. I hadn't started working on the detailed hourly reports for Wanda Taylor yet. I was dreading it.

I turned the radio on low and listened to some jazz on NPR. I needed coffee. There was a convenience store not far away, and I decided to drive over there and get some. Then I decided to call Juliet first. It was late, but I hadn't talked to her in a while.

She answered on the second ring.

"Hello?"

"It's me," I said.

"Nicholas, I've been worried sick. Are you all right?"

"I'm OK."

"You sound tired," she said.

"I'm OK. How is everything there?"

"I want you to come home."

"I know."

"Well?"

"I told Wanda Taylor I would try to find her father's killer. So that's what I aim to do."

"Are you having any luck?"

"Only bad. I'm sitting across the street from his widow's house right now. Maybe that'll turn into something."

"You'll come home for Thanksgiving, won't you?"

"I don't know. When is it?"

"It's next Thursday, goofy. Brittney's coming home for the whole four-day weekend."

"I might still be working on the case," I said.

"You couldn't take a couple of days off, to be with your family?"

"Wanda's dying. If I take a couple of days off, she might never find out what she wants to know."

Silence. I kept expecting umpteen kinds of hell again, but Juliet kept her cool this time.

"I heard The Zombie struck again," she said. "Just last night."

"He's on a roll," I said. "But they'll catch him soon."

"How do you know that?"

"He's starting to go to the well too often. Eventually he's going to screw up. Most serial killers do. They get cocky, and then they get careless. All it takes is one mistake."

"I just hope *you're* not making a mistake."

"What do you mean?"

"Nothing. It's late. I need to go. I have to get up early in the—"

"I've been thinking about something," I said.

"What's that?"

"I met a guy down here, a lounge singer. I went to his apartment one night and showed him some guitar licks."

"You were playing the guitar?"

"Not very well. The thing is, he said I would make a really good teacher."

"And you're thinking about that?"

"I called a music store yesterday, asked how much they charged for guitar lessons. Thirty-five bucks for half an hour. Can you believe that?"

"You would go to work for a music store?"

"I was thinking more along the lines of doing it on my own, maybe renting a little teaching studio somewhere. Anyway, it's something to think about."

"I think it sounds great. Anything that'll keep you here at home."

"Sure. So we'll talk about it when I get back."

"OK."

I still had no intention of ever teaching the guitar, but pretending to consider it seemed to be a healthy relationship remedy at the moment.

"I love you," I said. At least that part was the truth.

"I love you too, Nicholas."

We hung up, and I drove to the gas station to get a cup of coffee.

CHAPTER TWENTY-SIX

I was still wearing the sweaty mechanic getup, so I went to the restroom and freshened up a bit and changed clothes. When I came out, I asked the clerk if he would mind making some fresh coffee.

"You got money?" he said.

"Of course I have money. How else am I going to buy a cup of coffee?"

"There's half a pot on the burner over there. Go ahead and get yourself a cup. Free."

I glanced over at the coffee setup. There was half a pot of what looked like tar.

The clerk had seen me go into the restroom. He'd seen me stay in there awhile and come out with clean clothes and a shaved face. He thought I was some kind of hobo. He thought I lived like that all the time. I pulled a twenty out of my pocket and slapped it on the counter.

"I want some fresh fucking coffee," I said. "And I don't have all night. You want to make it for me, or you want me to make it myself? If I have to make it myself, you're not going to have a job tomorrow."

He pushed his glasses back on the bridge of his nose, got up from the wooden stool his fat ass had been parked on, and waddled over and started building a pot of coffee. While it was brewing, I flipped through the latest edition of *People* magazine. It reminded me how much I didn't miss the limelight.

Fame can suck. I've been there, so I know. You can end up sacrificing a good bit of your sanity in exchange for some money and adulation, and it's never worth the trade. I've seen too many casualties through the years. It can eat you alive, especially if you start buying into the hype. If you ever start believing your own press, good or bad, you're done.

I stood there and pitied the beautiful people until the fat, rude clerk said, "The coffee's ready."

I grabbed the largest size cup from a stack and filled it and put a lid on it. Walked to the counter, paid for the coffee and a 3 Musketeers bar, and left the store. The clerk didn't say anything to me, and I didn't say anything to him.

I drove back to Pamela Wade's house and parked in the same spot across the street. There was a white van parked in front of the house next door to Pamela's. It hadn't been there before. It was blocking a fire hydrant, so I figured whoever owned it didn't plan on leaving it there for long. I jotted down the tag number.

The clock rolled over to 12:01. It was Friday now. Less than a week until Thanksgiving. I sat there and sipped on my extremely large cup of coffee and listened to NPR some more. The jazz program had ended, and they were replaying an interview with an author named Laura Lippman. She lived in New Orleans part of the time, reminding me I needed to get down there one of these days and visit some old friends. And eat some crawfish. You just can't get it anywhere else.

Thinking about New Orleans made me hungry. I was starving. I unwrapped my candy and took a bite. It tasted good with the coffee. I took another bite, and a guy came out of Pamela Wade's front door and walked toward the white van. He wore bell-bottom jeans and a muscle shirt and flip-flops. Long curly blond hair and a mustache. He looked to be from a decade I'd tried to forget a long time ago. I wondered if the back of his van had been fitted with velour couches and an eight-track tape deck and a minibar.

Maybe this guy was a drug dealer. I would have bet dollars to 3 Musketeers bars he was selling something. Pamela had admitted to occasional marijuana use, so maybe it was that. Or maybe something harder. Cocaine or heroin. Or maybe he was just a friend, stopping by for a casual midnight blow job or something.

I was thinking about following him, but he didn't leave. Not then. He opened the passenger's side door and got something from under the seat and stuffed whatever it was into one of his front pockets. He slammed the door shut and walked back into the house.

I decided to take a chance. I called myself on the prepaid cell phone, and left the line open. I tore about eight inches of duct tape from the roll I'd bought at Kmart and stuck it to the side of my shirt. I climbed out of my car, looked around, trotted over to the van. I opened the same door hippie boy had opened. It hadn't been locked when he opened it, and it wasn't locked now. I smelled marijuana and just a hint of a woman's perfume. I felt under the seat, but he had taken all of whatever had been hidden there. The back of the van was just a metal shell. No couches. No strobe lights or disco balls or anything. I peeled the duct tape off my shirt and used it to secure the prepaid phone to a little crevice between the seats. Now I could use my regular phone to listen in on whatever happened inside the van.

I crept back to the Ford Focus and sat there and took some deep breaths. My heart was trying to punch its way out of my chest. I tried to relax. I ate the rest of my chocolate and drank my coffee and listened to NPR. An hour later, the seventies poster child came back out, and this time Pamela Wade was with him. I assumed it was her. I'd never seen a photograph of her, but the age was right.

Mid to late forties, a little younger than me. She wore a white peasant blouse and tight cutoff shorts. She was barefoot. The hippie guy was a lot younger than her. For a minute I thought maybe he was her son, but when they got to the curb they leaned against the van and embraced and kissed. It wasn't the kind of kiss a mother gives a son. It was a lover's kiss, long and passionate. When it finally ended, they hugged some more and then the guy got into the van and started it. Pamela stood there and waved as he drove away, and then she walked back inside.

Just because they were lovers didn't mean he wasn't a drug dealer, and it didn't mean he wasn't involved in Phineas Carter's death. I started my engine. I let him get to the end of the block, and then I pulled out and followed him. I figured Pamela was in for the night now, and I didn't think there would be any more activity at the house. Whatever Pamela Wade had wanted—sex, drugs, rock and roll, maybe all of the above—Van Man had delivered it.

He drove over to A1A and headed north along the coastline. The Atlantic Ocean was to our right. I could hear it through the bullet holes in my passenger's side window. Hotels lined the street to our left. Nice places with specialty restaurants and valet parking.

I allowed two or three cars to stay between us at all times. I didn't want Van Man to think he was being followed. Of course, he might have thought that anyway, depending on what type of drugs he was into. He might have thought government agents were watching him all day every day.

He pulled to the ocean side of the highway and braked to a stop beside a parking meter. I drove on by. If I had stopped, he would have made me for sure. I took a left on Seventeenth, turned into an alley, and waited there for a couple of minutes. I turned around, went back out to A1A, and took a right. I drove south about a quarter of a mile, made a U-turn, and pulled to the beachside curb. Now there was a good distance between us.

I could see the white van clearly, but I doubted he would notice the black Ford Focus.

I took a sip of my coffee. It was cold, but it still had the caffeine I needed. A pack of smokes would have been nice. I could remember lighting one after another and guzzling what seemed like gallons of coffee in an effort to stay alert on nights like this. It worked, but it was a slow form of suicide. The cigarettes, anyway. I read somewhere that coffee is actually good for you. I took another bitter, lukewarm drink, hoping it was true.

I opened my netbook. All the hotels along the strip had Wi-Fi, so it was easy to pick up a signal. I ran the van's tags and saw that a man named Daniel Chard owned the vehicle.

Dan the Van Man, I thought.

He was thirty-five years old. Never married, no financial stuff, no arrests. He had a clean record, but for some reason I couldn't imagine this guy teaching Sunday school. I figured he was into something. He'd just never gotten caught.

I closed the computer, and a few minutes later a blue SUV pulled to the curb in front of Dan's van. The driver got out. He was short and fat, and he wore a dark suit with a shirt and tie and sunglasses. Dark hair, dark skin. He walked around to the passenger's side and opened the back door. A very attractive young woman climbed out. She also had dark hair and dark skin. She looked young, maybe not even eighteen. She wore tight jeans and a nylon windbreaker, and her silky black hair hung to her waist.

The guy took her by the arm and escorted her to the white van. He opened the passenger's side door for her, and she climbed in. He walked around to the driver's side and talked to Dan through the window. I took my camera out of the bag and snapped some pictures, and I listened to their conversation with my makeshift cell-phone bug.

"I thought you said there were two of them," Dan said.

"The other one backed out at the last minute," the dark guy said.

"Fuck. Then I'm only paying half."

"Whatever. You got the money?"

"Yeah."

Thirty seconds or so ticked off, and then Dan handed the dark guy an envelope.

"Have a good night," the dark guy said.

"Later."

The dark guy walked to his SUV, climbed in, and drove away. Dan's taillights came on, but the van didn't move.

"What's your name?" Dan said.

"Veronica," the girl said.

"Let me see your driver's license."

"Why?"

"To make sure you're old enough," Dan said.

"You don't trust me?"

"No."

I heard some shuffling, and then Veronica said, "There. Now do you believe me?"

"Cool. You ready to do this thing?"

"I'm ready. This is exciting. This is, like, my dream, you know? I'm so nervous."

"Don't worry about it," Dan said. "You'll do fine."

The van pulled away from the curb.

I followed.

CHAPTER TWENTY-SEVEN

I tailed the van to a neighborhood several miles away. Once we were off the highway, I killed my headlights and followed at a distance. There was nothing but dead air on my cell phone. Dan and Veronica weren't talking.

The van pulled into a driveway, and a garage door opened remotely as I second-geared it past the house. There was a playground across the street. I eased to the curb and parked in front of it, hoping Dan hadn't seen me in his side-view mirror. He steered the van into the garage, and a few seconds later the motorized door came back down and mated flush with the concrete pavement.

On my phone, I heard the rumble of the van's engine stop abruptly.

"You smoke weed?" Dan said.

"Sure."

"I have some killer shit a friend brought me from Hawaii. I think it might help you loosen up a little."

"OK."

I heard the van's doors open, and then slam shut. Dan and Veronica were going inside. Now my little makeshift audio bug was useless. It was in the van, and the people I wanted to hear were in the house.

A light came on in the front room. I wanted to know what was going on behind those doors. I wanted to be a fly on the wall, but it wasn't going to happen. The only way for me to possibly watch them was to sneak around the outside of the residence and hope they were stupid enough to be in a room with a naked window. It didn't seem likely, not likely enough for me to risk getting caught creeping the place.

I shut my engine off. Locked the doors and cracked the windows. I was exhausted. Occasionally, a bright light would explode in my peripheral vision. Like a camera flash. It was a hallucination, brought on by sleep deprivation. I'd experienced it before. Nobody really knows why you need sleep, only that you do. To go without it for very long is detrimental to your mental and physical health. I put my seat back and closed my eyes. Just ten minutes, I told myself.

In my dream I walked into a convenience store to get a cup of coffee.

"We don't serve bums here," the clerk said.

"I'm not a bum. I have money."

"You're a loser. You're an alcoholic and a heroin addict. You lost your investigator's license, and you can't even play the guitar anymore."

"I'm working," I said. "I have ten thousand dollars in the bank."

"All you do is watch TV and drink beer and eat pork rinds. You're a total waste of a human being."

"Are you going to make some fresh coffee, or am I going to have to make it myself? If I have to make it myself, I'm going to saw the top of your head off and scoop your brain out."

I got dizzy and fell backward and started falling, falling, falling, into a bottomless pit of cold, black tar.

"You're a loser," the clerk said.

I was still in the store, but the store had morphed into a diner and the clerk had morphed into Rex from *Time Traveling Zombie Bikers from Darkest Hell.*

"Where's Charlie?" I said.

"Charlie don't work here anymore."

Rex turned and flipped something with a spatula. Six other guys, all of them appearing to be sleep-deprived and deathly ill, were sitting at the counter staring at me. I looked down at myself, and I was naked. I was naked except for the silver sheriff's badge pinned to my left nipple.

"You boys own those bikes out there?" I said.

The six guys grunted and nodded.

"We got no use for Dan the Van Man," I said.

"You're a loser," Rex said.

The sickly fellows rose from their stools. I hoped they were going to leave, but I knew they weren't. They surrounded me and started ripping me to pieces with their teeth.

I woke up gasping for air. I switched the ignition on and lowered the electric windows all the way. A cool tropical breeze washed over me, and in a couple of minutes I no longer felt as though I might be having a cardiac event.

I wiped the sweat from my forehead with my shirt. I wanted a drink. I wanted to get drunk and go back to the little island and pass out for two days this time.

I looked at my watch. It was almost three o'clock. I'd slept for over an hour.

The light in the front room was still on, so I figured Dan and Veronica were still in the house.

"Excuse me, sir."

A guy stuck his head in my passenger's side window. He must have been sleeping in the park. His eyes were bloodshot, his hair and beard thunderstorm gray. I could smell the whiskey on his breath.

"What do you want?" I said.

"I was on my way to Miami to see my mother in the hospital, and my car broke down. It's right down the street, just a few blocks away, but I can't afford to get it fixed. I'm trying to get together enough money for a bus ticket, and I was wondering if you had a couple of dollars you could spare."

I knew he was full of crap. Panhandlers are always having car trouble, and their mothers are usually in the hospital.

"You got a bottle?" I said.

"Me? No sir. I never touch the stuff."

"I'll give you ten bucks for one drink."

"Show me the money," he said.

"Show me the bottle."

He reached into his jacket and pulled out a pint of bourbon. It was about three-quarters full. It was an off-brand. Cheap rotgut.

He stared at me with those glassy red eyes. "You said one drink, right?"

"I'll give you twenty for the whole bottle," I said.

"All the liquor stores are closed. I won't be able to buy any more till in the morning."

"You can take a big swig before you hand it over. And there's a house not far from here where you can go crash for the night."

"What kind of house?"

"The abandoned kind. There's a guy staying there, but I'm sure he'll welcome the company. And I'm sure he won't mind sharing some of his booze."

He uncapped the bottle and took a drink. "Let's see the money," he said.

I handed him a twenty-dollar bill, and he handed me the bottle. I told him how to get to the squatter's house on Drake Upton's street. It was all I could do to keep from laughing. I knew how much the squatter would enjoy a houseguest. It was my way of paying the son of a bitch back for double-crossing me.

"You want to make another twenty?" I said.

"I'm not gay, if that's what you're thinking."

"Trust me. That's not what I'm thinking. I just want you to walk around the perimeter of that house over there and tell me if there are any windows you can see into."

"That's it?"

"Yeah. I'll give you half the money now and half when you get back."

"I can do that."

I gave him ten dollars. He looked both ways, crossed the street, and walked onto Dan the Van Man's yard.

CHAPTER TWENTY-EIGHT

I uncapped the bottle and took a sip of the bourbon. It was harsh, like liquid fire. I wondered if the panhandler had emptied out the liquor and replaced it with paint thinner. I still had some coffee in my enormous cup from the convenience store, so I poured some of the whiskey in and swirled it around and gave it a try. It wasn't bad. It was tolerable. I added some more of the rotgut and took a couple of sips and wished more than ever that I had a cigarette. It had been over two years since I'd smoked one, but at that moment my cravings were as bad as the day I quit. It never leaves you. Once an addict, always an addict.

I had a decent buzz going by the time the panhandler came back. He walked to my window and clocked me in the jaw with his fist. It was a sucker punch. It took me totally by surprise. I saw stars, and a wave of nausea washed over me. He reached in and tried to latch onto me, and I leaned over and opened the glove compartment and grabbed the .45 and pointed it at his face.

"Hit me again," I said. "Go ahead, motherfucker."

"You set me up," he said.

"What are you talking about?"

"There's a fucking security camera over the door to the shed, around back. I didn't notice the damn thing until it was too late. Now they got my face on film. I don't like that shit."

"I didn't know," I said.

"You going to keep pointing that gun at me?" he said.

"You going to punch me anymore?"

"No."

I put the pistol away. He backed out of the window. We were both breathing hard.

"Did you see anything?" I said.

"Yeah, I saw plenty. I saw a young girl sucking some long-haired motherfucker's balls. That's what I saw. They had bright lights on, and a camera set up on a tripod. They're making a goddamn pornographic movie over there."

So that's what they were up to. The fat guy in the SUV had delivered an *actress* to the hippie guy. She was probably a runaway, and they probably weren't even paying her for what she was doing. They were probably calling it a screen test or some such bullshit, with the promise of more work if she performed well enough. It was a common scam. Hippie boy gets his rocks off for cheap, and he gets a new skin flick for his website to boot.

My daughter was about the same age as Veronica. It made me sick to think about it.

"You did good," I said to the panhandler. "I'm going to give you a bonus for your troubles."

I handed him a twenty dollar bill. Altogether I'd given him fifty bucks for some bad liquor and five minutes worth of surveillance work.

"Appreciate it," he said. "Sorry I hit you. I guess I just lost my head there for a minute."

"Yeah. All right, man. Take care."

He scratched his beard. "Think I could have one more drink?"

I handed him the bottle. He took a drink and handed it back. He walked down the street and took a left, heading in the direction of the abandoned house I'd told him about.

Now I had something to work with. Dan the Van Man was into exploiting young women, and Pamela Wade was into Dan the Van Man. No telling what else they were into together. Phineas Carter might have gotten in their way at one point, and getting in their way might have gotten him killed.

I wanted to walk around to the back of the house and snap some pictures of Dan and Veronica in the act, but I didn't want to get caught on the security camera. I decided it was pointless to wait around. I stashed the whiskey bottle in the glove compartment alongside the .45, and I was about to start my engine and go find a room for the night when someone pressed the cold steel barrel of a shotgun against my ear.

My left hand was on the steering wheel, and my right hand was on the ignition. I didn't move.

"What are you doing?" the guy with the shotgun said.

"I'm not doing anything. I was just leaving."

"Why were you snooping around my house a few minutes ago?"

"I wasn't."

"Well somebody sure as fuck was."

"It wasn't me."

"Get out of the car," he said. "Keep your hands where I can see them."

I got out of the car. I kept my hands where he could see them. It was Dan. Tight jeans, no shirt, no shoes. His face was tense, his eyes wild. He was high on something. Something other than pot. He pointed the shotgun at my chest. It was a twelve-gauge pump. One squeeze of the trigger and my heart would be hamburger.

"There was a derelict walking around out here," I said. "That's who cased your house. He went that way."

I didn't really rat the old guy out. I pointed in the opposite direction of the way he'd gone.

"We're going to go inside now and have a little talk," Dan said. "I'll look at the playback on my security camera, and if what you're saying is true I'll let you go. OK?"

"Do I have a choice?" I said.

"Not really."

He motioned for me to walk toward the house, and he followed a few steps behind with the gun pointed at my back.

When we got to the front door, I said, "You want me to open it?"

"Yeah."

I opened the door and walked in. The hard rock band AC/DC was blasting from a pair of Bose speakers. There were some professional photography lights on stands, and a camera on a tripod. Just like the panhandler had said. Veronica was sitting on the couch in a white terrycloth bathrobe. She was crying.

"It's all right, baby," Dan said. "I just need to talk to this asshole for a few minutes."

"Can you take me home first?" she said.

"We're not done with your audition yet. You're not going to bail on me now, are you?"

"I don't like guns. I want to go home."

"Everything's going to be all right," Dan said. "You, asshole, sit on that chair over there."

He motioned toward an armless wooden chair with padding on the seat. It was a dining-room chair, but he had it in front of a computer setup in the corner. I walked over and sat on it. The computer was turned off. I was facing the wall, but I could see Dan and Veronica in the monitor screen. I could see their reflections. Dan was still holding the shotgun. Veronica was still crying. I was still feeling a little dizzy and nauseated from being punched in the jaw. And from the lack of sleep and the cheap liquor. I felt lousy. I wasn't in the mood for any of this bullshit.

I kept waiting for Dan to retrieve his security tape, and he kept not doing it. Those bugged-out, bloodshot eyes of his made me nervous.

"Open that suitcase over there," Dan said to Veronica.

"What?"

"Just do it."

Veronica got up and walked to the other side of the sofa. There was a beat-up brown leather suitcase placed decoratively beside the end table. There were some old books on top of the table, and some distressed maps or nautical charts or something in the bin beneath it. Veronica picked up the suitcase and set it on the couch.

"This?" she said.

"Yeah. Open it."

She opened it. "Oh my god," she said.

The suitcase was full of sex equipment. Like the drawer under the bed on Jim Ballard's boat.

"Take one of those scarves and tie asshole's hands behind his back," Dan said.

"What are you going to do?"

That's when Dan lost it. His demeanor changed abruptly. In the monitor screen, I saw him walk over and slap Veronica in the face with his palm. He hit her hard. It was loud. It sounded like a handclap.

"Did I stutter, bitch? Now take one of those fucking scarves and tie asshole's hands behind his back like I fucking told you to."

I wanted to wring his neck. "I thought you were going to look at your security video and then let me go," I said.

"Shut the fuck up."

I didn't know what Dan had in mind, but he was hyped up on something, and I didn't trust him one bit with that shotgun. He looked like the kind of guy who might kill Veronica and me and then kill himself.

"Asshole, turn the chair around this way," he said.

I got up and turned my chair around 180 degrees. I sat back down. Now I was facing the front of the room. Veronica walked around and tied my wrists behind my back with a black scarf.

"Now take his shoes and socks off," Dan said. He hesitated for a moment. "And then his pants and underwear."

CHAPTER TWENTY-NINE

Veronica removed my shoes and socks. Then, with a series of quick, successive jerks, she managed to yank my pants and underwear past the chair seat and off my legs. Now I was naked from the waist down.

"You're making a big fucking mistake," I said, loud enough to be heard above the stereo. "You better let me go. Now. People are going to be looking for me. My car's right outside."

"Tie his ankles to the legs of the chair," Dan said.

Veronica took two more scarves from the suitcase and tied my ankles to the legs of the chair. In the meantime, Dan repositioned the light stands and the camera. He got everything the way he wanted it, and then he pulled a ball gag out of the suitcase and strapped it around my head. He picked up the shotgun again.

"Now maybe you'll shut the fuck up," he said. He turned to Veronica. "Get him hard."

"You're fucking crazy, aren't you?" she said. "You're fucking insane."

"You better get that motherfucker's dick hard before I blow your goddamn brains all over this room."

Veronica locked eyes with the madman. Her lips were trembling. I could tell she wanted to say something, but she didn't. She knelt down in front of me and started raking her fingers along the inside of my thighs. Inexplicably, I felt myself starting to get aroused. There was nothing sexy about any of it. It was a physiological response to a stimulus, nothing more and nothing less. I never thought it was possible for a man to be raped by a woman, but now I knew it was. Veronica did some things with her tongue, and before long I had a full-fledged erection.

Dan was standing behind the camera. He'd leaned the twelve-gauge against the sofa. "Fuck him," he said.

Veronica didn't want this any more than I did. In a way, we were both being raped. Fat tears rolled down her cheeks as she disrobed and slid warmly and wetly on top of me.

Threads of drool dangled from the corners of my mouth. The ball gag stimulated salivation, and at the same time made it difficult to swallow. Dan had taken the camera off the tripod and was walking around with it now, getting some close shots of our faces and some close shots of our engorged and engaged genitals.

I tried to say, *You're going to die, you son of a bitch*, but it came out sounding like incomprehensible gibberish. Dan just laughed at me.

"What are you mad about?" he said. "You're getting laid, aren't you? You should be paying me for this shit."

Veronica kept gliding gently up and down on me. She was young and wet and tight, and for a second I thought I was going to come. I fought it, and eventually the sensation subsided.

Dan was lying on the floor with the camera angled up at us. He was laughing. The motherfucker was actually laughing. He was flying high and having a good time at our expense.

"That's nice," he said. "Keep grinding on it, baby."

Veronica was moaning. She wrapped her arms around me and leaned in close.

She whispered in my ear. "I tied a slipknot," she said.

When Dan got up and walked back to the tripod, she reached around and tugged on the scarf securing my wrists. I felt it loosen. In a single fluid motion, I wriggled free and pushed Veronica out of the way and tilted the chair back and slipped out of the ankle restraints. Dan went for the shotgun. As his right hand gripped the stock, I clobbered him over the head with the chair I'd been tied to. A six-inch gash opened on the top of his skull.

He collapsed to the floor with a thud. I thought he was finished, but whatever drug he'd taken somehow kept him animated. He rose and swung at me wildly, and one of the punches caught my left eye. I staggered back. I was dazed. He went for the shotgun again. He picked it up and crunched a shell into the chamber. He wanted to shoot me, but his eyes weren't tracking right. They were glazed and unfocused. His vision had been affected by the blow to the head.

Bright red blood trickled down his face in streams. I couldn't believe he was still standing. He wobbled and squinted and brought the barrel of the gun up level with my chest. A split second before he squeezed the trigger and blew a hole the size of a saucer in the opposite wall, I dove to my left and went crashing into one of the light stands. The stand toppled and the bulb exploded. It probably made a hell of a noise, but I didn't hear any of it. The shotgun blast had deafened me.

Dan one-handedly jacked another shell into the chamber. He started looking around the room, as if he didn't quite know where he was. Then it came to him. He snapped out of it. An expression of awareness washed over his face. He turned the gun on me again.

Before he got the barrel lined up, before he pulled the trigger and blasted me to mincemeat, Veronica rushed in and stabbed him in the belly with a steak knife. She must have gone to the kitchen while Dan and I were busy trying to kill each other.

Dan nonchalantly glanced down at the knife handle sticking out of his gut. As if it were a minor annoyance. A beesting or something. Maybe he couldn't feel the pain, but the damage had been done. He coughed, and a thick wad of blood splattered on the floor in front of him. He dropped to his knees. His face looked the way a pizza looks before you throw the cheese on it and shove it into the oven. White and doughy and red all over. He aimed and fired at Veronica, and in an instant the left side of her head disappeared in a spray of blood and flesh and bone. She fell backward, dead before she hit the couch.

Dan was still alive, but he didn't have the strength or presence of mind to pump the shotgun again. He pointed it at my naked crotch and squeezed the trigger, but nothing happened. I ran forward and kicked him in the nose with the ball of my foot. I couldn't hear anything, but I felt the crunch. That was all it took. His eyes rolled back and he toppled forward.

His body slapped flush against the hardwood floor, pushing the steak knife deeper into his abdomen. The pointy end of the blade broke through the skin on his back, exposing about two inches of the blood-soaked steel.

I stood there heaving. The room looked like a slaughterhouse. I tore off the ball gag and tossed it aside. My eyeballs throbbed with every heartbeat, and my ears felt as though someone had stuffed wet rags into them. I could only faintly make out the heavy drums and guitars of Iron Maiden's "Fear of the Dark" coming from the stereo speakers. I walked over and yanked the plug out of the wall. Now there was silence, except for the constant ringing in my head. I found my pants and underwear and shoes and socks. I got dressed and threw Dan's camera on the floor and stomped it to pieces, and then I went to the garage and got my prepaid cell phone out of the van. The battery was dead. I walked back through the house and out the front door. I stopped and vomited on the lawn, and then I staggered across the street and got in my car and drove away from there as fast as I could.

CHAPTER THIRTY

I drove back to the convenience store by Pamela Wade's house, where I'd bought the coffee. The same clerk was on duty.

"What happened to you?" he said.

"Never mind. I need to use your phone."

"We're not allowed to let customers use the phone, sir. There's a pay phone right outside."

"All right. Give me change."

I slapped a dollar bill on the counter. He punched a code into the computerized cash register, and the drawer sprang opened and he handed me four quarters. I walked outside. The phone was on the right side of the building, by the freezer where they kept bags of ice for sale. It had been awhile since I'd used a pay phone. The price had gone up. When I was ten, local calls cost a dime. Now they were fifty cents. On average, the price had gone up a penny every year. It made me feel old. I loaded two quarters into the slot and dialed 911, and the coins immediately rattled back at me, down the chute to the change receptacle. Apparently you got a free phone call when someone was dead or dying or on fire or something. I probably knew that at one time.

"Emergency services," the dispatcher said. "Is this a real emergency?"

My hearing had started to come back, but everything still sounded muffled.

"There's been a double homicide," I said. "So I guess you could call it a real emergency. But there's no hurry. The dead people aren't going to get any deader."

"Is this a joke?"

"No."

I gave her Dan's address, and then clacked the receiver into its cradle. I knew the dispatcher would have a lock on the location I'd made the call from, so I didn't want to hang around. There was no reason for me to get tangled up in the investigation. I would have spent hours at the police station, and maybe years in court. It wasn't worth the hassle. Once the police walked into the horror show that was now Dan's house, it would be obvious what had happened. Dan and Veronica had been making a pornographic movie, and something had gone terribly wrong. She stabbed him, and then he shot her. End of story. No need for me to be involved.

I got in my car and drove over to Pamela Wade's house. I was beyond exhausted. Running on fumes. I wanted to go home. I was ready for this to be finished. I parked at the curb and marched to the front entrance and knocked. When nothing happened, I started stabbing at the button for the buzzer with one hand and pounding on the door with the other.

Finally, a light came on. The peephole went black, and a voice from inside said, "What the fuck do you want?"

"Pamela Wade?"

"Who wants to know?"

"Nicholas Colt. I talked to you on the phone before."

The door swung open. "I already told you everything I know. What the fuck are you doing at my house at five o'clock in the fucking morning?"

"Dan's not doing very well," I said.

"What?"

"Can I come in?"

She opened the door wider, and stepped back. She had a white bedsheet wrapped around her body, and she was barefoot. She looked as though she might have been going to a toga party. Her toenails were unpainted, and there were needle marks on the tops of her feet. Now I had a pretty good idea what Dan had gotten out of the van the first time I saw him. I stepped into the foyer, and Pamela closed the door.

"What the fuck are you talking about?" she asked.

"Can we sit down?"

"No, we can't fucking sit down. Now tell me what the fuck you're talking about before I call the cops and have your ass—"

"I'm really tired," I said. "And there's a good possibility you're going to prison. Your friend Danny boy was involved in what you might call the illicit side of the pornographic film industry—not that there's a legitimate side, as far as I'm concerned—and I'm pretty sure you knew about it. Maybe you were involved yourself. You're not going to call any cops. That's the last thing you want to do. I'm going to walk over there and sit on your couch, and you're going to go make a pot of coffee. Or, as you might like to say, a *fucking* pot of coffee. Then we're going to talk."

"What makes you think you can just waltz in here and start ordering me around?"

"I'm sorry. I didn't say please. *Please* go make a fucking pot of coffee."

If she'd been totally innocent, she would have booted me out then. Or maybe she would have called the cops. She didn't do either. She bit her lip and shook her head and stomped off into the kitchen. She didn't call my bluff. That told me she was guilty.

Of something.

I walked into the living room, switched on a lamp, and sat on the sofa. I sank into the cushions. It was a very comfortable couch. I must have nodded off, because the next thing I remember Pamela Wade was standing in front of me wearing a pair of melon-colored sweatpants and a tattered *Who Shot J.R.?* T-shirt. She'd pulled a long pair of socks onto her tracked-up feet.

"You want cream and sugar?" she said.

"Just black. Thanks."

She came back a couple of minutes later with two mugs. She handed me one of them, and then sat on the sofa beside me.

"OK, you got your coffee. Now what was it you wanted to talk to me about? Are you trying to tell me Dan is in some kind of trouble?"

"Yeah. The worst kind. He's dead."

She dropped her cup. It fell to the floor and shattered.

"What do you mean?" she said.

"He's dead. There's no other way to put it."

Tears welled in her eyes. "That's not possible. I just saw him awhile ago. You're lying. Why are you doing this to me?"

"Try to call him," I said. "Or better yet, drive on over to his house. You'll see half a dozen police cars and a bunch of yellow tape."

She lost it then. She stood, careful to avoid the puddle of coffee and the shards from the broken mug, and shouted, "Get out of here. Get out of my fucking house. You're lying. Just *go*!"

She fell to her knees in front of me and started sobbing into her hands.

I reached into my pocket and pulled out the bottle of whiskey I'd bought from the old derelict. "Here," I said.

She grabbed the bottle, uncapped it, took a big swallow. Like it was water.

"Easy," I said. "You could unclog drainpipes with that shit."

She was trembling. She didn't hand the bottle back. "Are you sure...Dan..."

"I'm sure. I'm very sorry. I know the two of you were close."

She was doing her best to pull herself together. "What happened?" she said.

"Like I told you on the phone, I was hired to find out who killed Phineas Carter. I'd decided to watch your place for a while. I really didn't have anywhere else to go. No other leads..."

I told her everything that had happened, except the part about me ending up a prisoner in Dan's house. I left that part out. I told her I had been parked on the street watching the place when I heard the gunshots. There was no reason to tell her that I had been tied to a chair and raped. I didn't tell her the whole truth, and I didn't tell her nothing but the truth, but I told her what she needed to know.

She took another swig from the whiskey bottle. "I can't believe this is happening," she said. "All we wanted was a better life."

"And you thought you could get it by exploiting young women?" I said.

"It wasn't supposed to turn out like this. We wanted to make enough money to move to Costa Rica. Buy a little surf shop. Just live peacefully."

"Who killed Phin?" I said.

She moved back to the couch and sat beside me. "I don't know," she said.

"I think you do know. I think you and Dan started having an affair, started making some plans, and it was easier to just get rid of Phin than to deal with divorcing him. I bet you and Dan used the life-insurance money to get your little porn operation underway. Huh? Is that how it went down?"

She started sobbing again. "No. Dan was involved with some pretty shady characters, but I swear I don't know anything about who killed Phineas. Yes, Dan and I were having an affair. And yes, we were making plans to move away. There was an insurance policy, but it never crossed my mind to kill my husband. I was going to file for divorce. I was just waiting for the right time, you know?"

"Do you think it might have crossed *Dan's* mind to kill your husband? I mean, how could it not have?"

"Dan was with me the night Phin was murdered. I was at Dan's place, and then I stopped and got a few things at Walmart and went home. That's when I found my husband with a bullet in his head. And now Dan's dead too. Oh my god, I just can't believe this is happening."

"Did the cops ever find out you were with your lover the night Phin was killed?"

"No. I just told them I went to the store. I'd used my debit card, and I had the receipt, so my whereabouts were well documented. Dan and I stopped seeing each other for a while after that, until the heat was off."

"You think one of Dan's acquaintances might have killed your husband?" I said. "Maybe someone Phin was familiar with as well?"

Her expression told me I might be on to something. She closed her eyes and wiped away the tears.

"Of course the thought occurred to me," she said. "Many times. But whenever I brought it up, Dan just told me not to worry about it. I don't know. I never pressed the issue, because knowing something like that can end up turning against you. It can get you killed."

"For some reason, I believe you," I said. "I'm going to have to report all this to the police, but you should be all right. I'm going to give them the tag number of the SUV I saw delivering Veronica to Dan earlier, and I'm going to give them a description of the man driving. Of course the cops will be around to talk to you. Just tell them the same thing you told me. And do me a favor."

"What's that?"

"Don't tell them about me. I'm going to make the call anonymously."

"Why?"

"It's a long story. Just pretend I don't exist."

"Why would I want to help you?"

"Because if you don't, I'm going to tell them about your other dirty little secret. Ever try to go cold turkey in a jail cell? It's not a very pleasant experience."

She clawed at her face. "All right. I won't tell them about you. I guess I can do that. I guess it doesn't matter. This is so fucked-up."

"Definitely," I said.

I took one last sip of coffee and got up to leave. Pamela tried to hand the bottle of bourbon back to me. I told her to keep it.

CHAPTER THIRTY-ONE

I tried to drive directly back to Key West, but I didn't make it. I was too tired. After staring at the road for thirty minutes and passing six or seven pink giraffes hitchhiking, I pulled off at a rest stop and slept in the car for four hours.

I made it back to my original hotel room Friday afternoon. I climbed into bed and slept several more hours, and when I woke up there was a message on my cell phone from Detective Craig P. Sullivan, Monroe County Sheriff's Office, Homicide Investigations Unit.

Sullivan wanted me to call him. I wondered how he expected me to do that, since I was supposedly dead.

I decided to call Wanda Taylor first. She answered on the first ring.

"Hello?"

"Hi, Wanda. It's Nicholas Colt."

"Nicholas. Oh my god, we thought you drowned. The Coast Guard was looking for you. Then the guy whose boat you were supposed to have fallen off of—"

"It's a long story," I said. "But right now, let me just tell you this: I'm pretty sure I know who killed Phineas Carter."

"Really? Has there been an arrest?"

"Not yet. I don't know *exactly* who killed him, but I have a very good lead to give to the police. They'll follow up on it. Eventually, a lot of people will be going to jail."

"Did it have to do with smuggling drugs, like you thought at first?"

"No. It had to do with greed and jealousy and sex for sale."

I told her everything I'd learned from my adventures with Daniel Chard and Pamela Wade. Again, I left out the part about me being captured and imprisoned and sexually assaulted. Nobody needed to know about that. Ever.

"So I guess it might be awhile before I find out who the actual triggerman was," Wanda said.

"It might be awhile, or we might never know. It just depends on how extensive the crime network is. At any rate, it's beyond the scope of my practice. I've already done way more than I should have, working without a license and all. I'm going to have to do some fancy tap dancing just to stay out of jail myself."

"I appreciate your efforts," Wanda said. "Do I owe you any more money?"

"No. In fact, I owe you some. I didn't use nearly all your ten thousand dollars."

"Call it a bonus, then. I don't want any money back."

"Are you sure?" I said.

"I'm sure. Thank you, Nicholas."

After we said good-bye, I sat there at the little desk in my room for a few minutes and debated over whether or not to call Detective Sullivan. I finally decided I didn't have much of a choice. If he didn't know I was alive already, he would find out eventually, and if I didn't call him now he might go harder on me later. I played his message again, and then punched in the number to call him back.

"This is Sullivan."

"Nicholas Colt," I said.

"So it's true. You are alive."

"Yeah. How did you know?"

"Robbie Asbury. He was in a coma for a while. When he came out of it, he said you were at the scene of the accident. I figured he dreamed it or something. I really didn't expect you to ever get the message I left on your cell."

"Did he tell you he took a couple of shots at me?" I said.

"No. He left that part out, but we did find a gun in the car. Interesting."

"I didn't think he recognized me," I said. "He'd only seen me that one time, at his and Alison's condo, and my appearance has changed pretty drastically since then."

"Sometimes coma-induced head injuries can conjure up revelations that a healthy brain would filter out. That's what I've heard, anyway. So what the hell happened? Jim Ballard said you jumped off his boat to go for a swim, and that—"

"Jim Ballard was full of shit. He knocked me out and threw me overboard. It was only by the grace of God and a school of dolphins that I ever made it back to shore alive."

"So you've been playing possum for the past three days?"

"I've had a bad case of amnesia," I said. "I'm just now starting to remember some things."

"Right."

"Work with me on this, Detective. I have a couple of pieces of information you might be interested in."

"The Coast Guard wasted a lot of man-hours and helicopter fuel looking for your ass, Colt. They're going to be mighty pissed when they find out—"

"Like I said. A bad case of amnesia."

I could hear him tapping a pencil on his desk. "I'm going to need you to come down to the station," he said. "Unless you would rather me send someone over to pick you up."

"What makes you think I'm still in Key West?"

"Are you?"

"Maybe. So that's how it's going to be? You're going to arrest me?"

"Maybe not. But I need you to come to the station anyway. I need to get your official statements on some things."

"What things?"

"Regarding the Alison Parker murder. We have the serial killer in custody."

"You caught The Zombie?" I said.

"Yeah. Haven't you figured it out yet? It was Robbie Asbury. No doubt about it."

"He confessed?"

"Let's just say we have all the evidence we need to convict him."

"What evidence?"

"It's no big secret. It's already been leaked to the media. We have forensics that conclusively link Robbie with another one of the slayings. The Roger Englehart case."

"Murder number six," I said. "The registered nurse who lived in St. Augustine. The body was found under a railroad bridge in Brunswick."

"I see you've done a little homework."

"Yeah."

"So that's it. We found several fingerprints on the plastic trash bags that had been wrapped around Englehart before he was dumped in the creek, and we found a couple of hairs on the corpse that didn't belong on the corpse. When Alison was killed, we combed the apartment for evidence, and of course Robbie's hairs and prints were all over the place. That's when we were able to match him with what we'd found on Englehart. Suddenly there was a common thread among three of the murders. It doesn't get much more open and shut than that."

"Robbie was married to Alison," I said. "And friends with Jim Ballard. He'd probably been on Jim's boat plenty of times."

"But he wasn't married to Roger Englehart," Sullivan said. "And they weren't buddies. The Englehart case is what's going to make all this come together in court. I promise you, Robbie Asbury is The Zombie. I'm one hundred percent sure of that."

"What about the forensics on the other murders attributed to The Zombie?"

"All the other corpses were clean. He only fucked up that one time, but that's all it's going to take. He probably even has alibis for a lot of the killings, as spread out as they were geographically. Most serial killers cover their tracks pretty well. But all it takes is one conviction, and we have solid evidence in the Englehart case. I'm pretty sure the DA's going to seek the death penalty with this one."

"All right. Well, I'll be happy to give you a statement. I'll be happy to help you in any way I can."

And that's when it hit me. That's why Sullivan wasn't going to arrest me. It wouldn't look good for one of his key witnesses to be facing criminal charges. I'd been the first person other than Robbie to see Alison's dead body lying on the floor of the apartment. There was that, and now Sullivan knew that Robbie had tried to shoot me, which augmented a violent profile the district attorney would be eager to exploit. When the time came, the prosecution would need a fine upstanding citizen to take the stand. Not a jailbird.

The evidence against Robbie seemed pretty conclusive, but I still wondered about what he'd said after he crashed that Caprice. *Jim Ballard is dead. I'm next.* He'd said it right before he passed out. Maybe he'd been delirious from the trauma. Maybe that was all there was to it, but I still wondered.

"It's getting late," Sullivan said. "Why don't you come on down first thing in the morning. I'll be in my office at eight o'clock."

"On a Saturday?"

"You think they give me weekends off around here? Get real."

"I'll be there," I said.

"Your car's in the impound lot. We can take care of that in the morning as well. And you said you might have some information for me. What's that all about?"

"I'll tell you tomorrow."

We disconnected, and I headed down to the lounge to have a drink. Relieved that Sullivan seemed to be on my side, relieved to be off the hot seat for now.

CHAPTER THIRTY-TWO

I sat at the bar and ordered an Old Fitz on the rocks. After the rotgut I'd procured from the panhandler the night before, it was like coming home to an old friend.

One more night in Key West, I told myself. One more night. I would stop and talk to Detective Craig P. Sullivan at eight o'clock in the morning, and from there hit the highway home. I'd come to Key West to find out who killed Phineas T. Carter, and I had a solid lead to give to the police now. My work was done. And, with Robbie Asbury in custody, it seemed The Zombie killings were solved as well. I was feeling pretty good about myself and the way things had turned out.

There were still some loose ends, like why Jim Ballard had tried to kill me. That was the big one. It had made sense back when I thought Jim was the one who'd killed Alison. If he'd been guilty of that crime, his motive for trying to get rid of me would have been a lot clearer. He might have thought I was getting too close to the truth. But Jim didn't kill Alison. Robbie did. Sullivan was sure of it. As far as I knew, Jim hadn't killed anyone, so I had no idea why he'd tried to kill me. I still hadn't figured that one out, and with Jim dead now, it wasn't likely I ever would.

It was happy hour, and there were quite a few people in the lounge. The bartender set a basket of peanuts in front of me. She had a great tan, a beautiful body, and perfect hair. The best money could buy. Her nametag said Josie.

"What time does the band start?" I said. There were amplifiers and microphone stands on the stage, and a drum kit draped with a sheet.

"Ten," she said. "They're really good. Can I get you another drink?"

"Sure. I'm celebrating." I pointed to her nametag. "Are you the lead singer?"

"Me?"

"Yeah. You know, Josie and the Pussycats."

"Who?"

I felt old again. "Never mind," I said.

She smiled and shrugged cutely. She scooped some ice cubes into a glass, grabbed the Old Fitz bottle, inverted it, and gave me a generous pour.

"What are you celebrating?" she said.

"Just being alive."

It probably sounded like a cliché to her. She had no idea how literal I was being. She gave me a thumbs-up and walked off to serve another customer.

I called Juliet and told her I would be home tomorrow night. She was very happy about that, and her excitement was contagious. I couldn't wait to see her. We'd only been apart for a few days, but it never took long to start feeling as though an integral part of me was missing. I guess that's what they call love.

A few minutes after Juliet and I said good-bye, my phone vibrated in my pocket. I thought maybe it was her calling me back, but the incoming number was unfamiliar. I answered the call.

"This is Nicholas Colt," I said.

"Hey, Nicholas!"

It was Wesley West. Maybe the last person on the planet I wanted to talk to.

"Hey, Wes," I said.

"What's up?"

"Nothing much. I'm heading home in the morning."

"Really?"

"Yeah, man. I'm outta here."

"I'm glad I caught you then. I was going to see if you wanted to come over and jam a little tonight."

That's what I was afraid of.

"I would like to," I said. "But I really can't. I still have to pack and everything. Sorry."

"Come on, man. You said you were going to show me the lead part to 'Dead Ringer.' You promised."

"Maybe next time. Listen, I really need to—"

"And you owe me four hundred dollars."

Damn. I'd forgotten about that. I still owed him four hundred on the pistol I'd bought from him. Fuck a duck.

"Can I mail you a check?" I said.

"You know better than that. I need the cash. I was trusting you to give it to me on Sunday, like you said you would."

"All right. I'll come over. But I can't stay long."

"Cool. I appreciate it, Nicholas. See you in a bit, then. I'll get the guitars tuned up."

I hung up. I didn't want to drive over there, but I decided not to let it put a damper on my good mood. I was going home tomorrow. That was all that mattered.

When Josie came around and asked if I wanted another drink, I told her to close out my tab.

"I thought you were going to stick around to hear the band," she said.

"I'll be back in a little while. I just need to run an errand real quick."

"You OK to drive?"

"I'm OK."

"I could get you a cup of coffee."

"I'm OK. Really."

She printed out a ticket, and I paid with cash. I left her a good tip.

I walked out to the parking lot. The wind had picked up, and the temperature had dropped. I decided to go back to the room and get a jacket. While I was there, I brushed my teeth and slapped on some aftershave. I did it to cover up the smell of the whiskey. I wasn't drunk, but I didn't want to give a cop probable cause to fuck with me if I happened to get pulled over for something. For one thing, I still had the .45 in the glove compartment, and it was illegal as hell.

I stopped at an ATM and withdrew four hundred dollars. It was almost nine o'clock by the time I got to Wesley West's apartment complex. I sat in the parking lot for a few minutes, thinking about everything that had happened over the past few days. It had all started when a young lady with a terminal illness decided to find her biological father. It amazed me sometimes, how one thing leads to another and how everything is interconnected. Kind of like *Seinfeld*. I wondered if the bartender at the hotel lounge would have gotten *that* reference. Probably not. I wondered if she would go home tonight and Google Josie and the Pussycats.

Might as well get this over with, I thought. I got out of my car, climbed the stairs to Wesley West's door, and knocked.

CHAPTER THIRTY-THREE

"Come on in, Nicholas. Good to see you, buddy."

He patted me on the back. He was acting as though we were old school chums who hadn't seen each other in a long time. All I wanted to do was give him his money and get the hell out of there.

The same two acoustic guitars were on stands near the television. Same sectional sofa, same round coffee table, same framed poster on the wall. Wesley had even set out another snack tray, with more of the pâté and crackers I'd enjoyed so much last time. Same fancy little knife. Same burgundy napkins. Déjà vu.

I pulled the cash out of my pocket and handed it to him. "Here you go," I said.

"Thanks. Grab a guitar and have a seat. You want a beer?"

"I really can't stay. Like I said, I still need to—"

"I'm making coffee, since that's what you wanted last time. It's almost done. Can I get you a cup?"

Wesley West was annoyingly persistent. I wanted to get out of there, but since he'd gone to all the trouble to start a pot of coffee, I decided it wouldn't hurt to have one cup. Maybe two, if it was that Kona stuff again.

"All right," I said. "I'll take a cup of coffee."

I picked up the Martin guitar and sat on the sofa. Wesley walked to the kitchen. I sat there and strummed a few chords, and then started trying to remember the lead solo to "Dead Ringer." I hadn't played it in years, and I was having some difficulty recalling exactly how it went.

"Hey, Wes," I shouted. "You wouldn't happen to have a copy of 'Dead Ringer' around here, would you?"

"Yeah, man. I have it on CD. I'll go get it in a second."

I set the guitar down, smeared some of the pâté on a cracker, and took a bite. It was very good. I loaded another cracker, stood and walked over to the Freak Willy tour poster hanging on the wall, just to kill some time while I waited for Wes.

It was the first time I'd taken a good look at the poster. There was a posed photograph of the band at the top, surrounded by a curlicue border. Wesley's hair was longer in the picture, and he was thinner. Beneath the band photo was a list of locations.

Greenville, SC
Savannah, GA
Durham, NC
Wilmington, NC
Lynchburg, VA
Key West, FL
Jupiter, FL
Cape Fear, NC

The cracker in my hand fell to the floor. When the Titanic slammed into that big chunk of ice in the North Atlantic Ocean over a hundred years ago, the captain of the ship couldn't have been any more stunned than I was at that moment. My ears got hot, and my pulse quickened. Acid rose in the back of my throat, a vile rendition of the eighty-proof Kentucky sour mash I'd consumed earlier.

The towns Wesley's band had played in were the exact same towns The Zombie had killed in. Brunswick was the only one missing.

He came from the kitchen carrying a cup of the expensive Hawaiian coffee in one hand and the "Dead Ringer" CD in the other. He saw me standing there looking at the poster.

I turned, and our eyes met.

He saw the expression on my face.

He knew that I knew.

I bolted for the door, but he tossed the CD case and the coffee cup aside and tackled me from behind before I could get my hand on the knob. I fell facedown to the floor. Before I could turn over and defend myself, he chopped me across the back of the neck with the side of his hand. It felt as though I'd been hit with a baseball bat. A branch of lightning crackled through my spinal column, and for a moment I was completely paralyzed.

Before I could even shout for help, Wesley grabbed one of the cloth napkins by the snack tray and stuffed it into my mouth. As the numbness in my arms and legs turned to tingling, and the tingling turned to pain, he dragged me by my feet to his bedroom and squeezed something out of a tube onto the palms of my hands. Something cold and slimy. He positioned me on my back and pressed my palms against the hardwood floor, and then he stood on the tops of my hands. He stood there until I thought the bones were going to crumble under the pressure. I tried to resist, but I was too weak. The blow to the back of the neck had done a number on me. I could feel my extremities now, but they were practically useless.

Wesley stepped away. I winced, the pain in my fingers over the next few seconds even more severe than when he'd been standing on them. The pain in my left hand was especially excruciating, because of all the surgeries and the resultant hardware. It felt as though someone was actively driving screws into my bones.

I tried to move, but I could not. My palms were glued to the floor.

He pulled my shoes and socks off next, and then he glued the lateral sides of my feet to the floor in the same manner. Now I was splayed out like some sort of specimen in a biology class.

"You're just a little too clever for your own good, Nicholas. I'm sorry it had to go down like this. I truly am. I like you. I like you a lot. But now you'll have to join the others. Such a shame, just when I thought our friendship was starting to gel. And damn it, I really did want to learn those licks on 'Dead Ringer.' Oh, well. Not meant to be, I guess."

He knelt down and opened his bottom dresser drawer. The drawer above it was the one with all the Vietnam stuff in it.

Damn, I thought. If I could only get my hands on that drawer.

But there was no use thinking about it. I was stuck to the floor like a fly on flypaper. I wasn't going anywhere.

There was an electric guitar on a stand in the corner, a Fender Telecaster. I noticed it because the pick guard was signed by an old friend of mine. Small world, I thought. I wondered how Eric had ever come in contact with the likes of Wesley West.

"Let's see now," Wesley said. "Ah. Here it is. I can't very well leave you glued to the floor when I'm finished, now can I?"

He pulled a quart-sized metal can of Sunnyside acetone out of the drawer. I'd used the same brand to clean some lawn mower parts one time. Juliet buys the stuff in an itty-bitty bottle with an itty-bitty paintbrush on the cap. She's not allowed to wear polish on her fingernails at the hospital, but she uses the acetone to remove the lacquer from her toes sometimes. It's a very useful solvent. Apparently Wesley West planned on using it to get me unstuck from the floor after performing his macabre surgical procedure on me.

"I bet you're wondering what I do with the brains," he said. "Everyone wonders that. I'm sure the FBI profilers think I keep them as trophies. Wouldn't that be a hoot? I could stuff each of them into a Mason jar full of formaldehyde, and then line the jars up on a shelf somewhere. Display them, like people do with big fish and moose heads. Of course, the carnival hawkers that call themselves *news reporters* have speculated since the beginning that I eat them. That's why those boneheads dubbed me The Zombie in the first place. Well, for once, the talking heads were right. You know that meaty paste on the snack tray that's so good on the little crackers?"

I turned my head to the side and started retching. I wanted to vomit, but I couldn't. Not with that cloth napkin stuffed so deeply into my mouth. I would have aspirated and drowned.

Of all the insane motherfuckers I'd come up against in my career as a private investigator, this one took the cake. He not only made pâté with his victims' brains, he served the ghastly preparation to guests.

He had served the ghastly preparation to *me.*

What Wesley West had done was beyond despicable. I no longer considered him a human being. He was a monster, pure and simple.

"I rarely get the chance to talk about these things to anybody," he said. "So when I do get the chance, it's kind of nice. Therapeutic, in a way. People are social animals. We need to talk to each other sometimes. Discuss things. Bat things around. Take Jim Ballard, for instance. He was a good talker."

Wesley kept rooting through the dresser drawer as he rambled on.

"Jim told me a lot of things," he continued. "Of course, I encouraged him a bit with a cigarette lighter and a pair of pliers. Jim killed a man. Did you know about that? Actually, he killed two men. The first was a guy named Phineas Carter, who had subleased Alison Palmer's condominium. Jim claimed it was an accident, but

I'm not so sure. I guess we'll never know now. Look, I even have the gun he did it with."

He reached into the drawer and produced what appeared to be a .38-caliber revolver. It was rusty and caked with sand.

"I haven't had a chance to clean it up yet. Nice gun, though. I had to yank three of Jim's fingernails out before he told me where it was buried. Phineas Carter never did anything to Jim, nothing that I could discern. Such a waste. Carter was just in the wrong place at the wrong time. It's really an intriguing story of jealousy and obsession. I'll have to tell you all about it sometime."

Wesley stopped ferreting. He stood abruptly and slammed the drawer shut with his foot.

"I must have left my little saw in the car," he said. "I could have sworn I put it back in the drawer. Anyway, it's been nice chatting with you. I wish there was a way you could participate in the conversation, but I'm afraid you'll be a bad boy and scream for help if I allow that to happen. This is the first time I've had to do this in my own house, so naturally I'm a little nervous about it. I hope you understand."

I grunted frantically.

"What's that?" Wesley said. "You promise not to shout if I take the rag out of your mouth? I don't know. I'm not sure I should trust you."

He opened the drawer again, reached in and pulled out a utility knife. He pushed the slide forward with his thumb, and the razor-sharp blade emerged with a click.

"I'm going to pull that napkin out now, and if you call for help I'm going to cut your tongue out. Do we have an understanding? Is it a deal?"

I nodded. He reached down and yanked the cotton cloth out of my mouth and tossed it aside.

I sucked in a wheezy, deep breath, and then coughed it out violently. "You're a sick motherfucker," I said.

"You better watch your tongue, Nicholas. If you want to keep it."

"I'm going to die anyway. What's the difference?"

"The difference is in how slow and how painful. Anyway, I don't know what I'm so worried about. It's not likely anyone is going to hear you, even if you do scream. The insulation is pretty good here, and the apartment below us has been vacant for some time now."

"Why did Jim Ballard kill Phineas Carter?" I said.

It was the reason I'd come to Key West in the first place. I wanted to know.

"Oh, yes. Let's talk about that for a minute. Like I said, it's a tantalizing tale of jealousy and obsession."

I figured there might be a connection between Jim Ballard and Daniel Chard. For one thing, they seemed to share an affinity for adult toys and bondage tools. All that kinky sex equipment. Maybe it was just a coincidence, but I figured there might be a connection. Maybe Jim had been part of the porn ring.

It took Wesley about ten minutes to tell the whole story. He told me what Jim Ballard had told him.

As it turned out, I had it all wrong.

CHAPTER THIRTY-FOUR

Alison Palmer had signed on with a traveling nurse company, and had moved to St. Augustine to get away from Jim Ballard. Before that, she had threatened Jim with a restraining order if he ever came near her again. Jim went along with it for a while, but eventually the imposed separation drove him bananas. He couldn't stand it anymore. He went to Alison's apartment one evening, and found Phineas Carter there in her place.

After talking to him for a while, Jim was satisfied that Phin wasn't Alison's new boyfriend or anything; but, he came back later, drunk, and tried to force Phin into telling him where Alison had moved to. He tried to force him by putting a gun to his head. Phin said he didn't know Alison's new address, said he sent the payment for his rent to Red Parrot Realty every month.

According to Jim, he didn't mean to blow Phin's brains out. The gun just went off.

Jim buried the revolver on his way back to Jake's Key West Saloon, where he'd been drinking before he returned to Phin's apartment. Jim had left his tab open at Jake's, which gave him a fairly solid alibi during the police investigation. According to the starting time and ending time on the receipt, Jim had never left the club.

Jim didn't know it at the time, but while all that was going on, Alison was busy meeting the love of her life up in St. Augustine.

Robbie Asbury and Alison Palmer first met on the beach one morning, soon after Alison left Key West. It was love at first sight. They were together for a few days, and then Robbie had to leave for a weekend gig out of town. That was all he told Alison, that it was out of town. He had agreed to sub for the drummer of a band called Blue Waves, and the job just happened to be at Jake's Key West Saloon. Jim Ballard just happened to be there having a late-morning beer when Robbie came in to set up his drums. Jim helped Robbie carry some things in, and one thing led to another, and eventually Jim overheard Robbie on his cell phone leaving Alison a voice mail. When Robbie left the phone unattended for a minute, Jim scrolled through and found Alison's address in St. Augustine.

Now Jim knew where she was. He confronted Robbie later that afternoon, told him that he and Alison were engaged. It was a lie, but that's what he told him. He insisted that Robbie stay away from Alison, or there would be hell to pay.

Later that night at the club, one of the bartenders told Robbie that Jim was full of shit. Jim and Alison had never been engaged, she said, and Alison had moved away because Jim had become physically abusive. Alison had left Key West because she was afraid of Jim Ballard.

Now Robbie was worried. He had a feeling Jim was on his way up to St. Augustine to find Alison. After playing the final set at Jake's, Robbie climbed into his truck and headed that way.

It was an eight-hour drive, and when he got to Alison's apartment Jim Ballard was indeed there.

But so was another man.

Robbie had carried a baseball bat with him to Alison's door, thinking he would at least intimidate Jim with it. Robbie heard scuffling, walked in, and saw Jim on the floor wrestling with a shirtless man in white scrub pants. An instant before the shirtless man plunged a knife blade into Jim Ballard's chest, Robbie gripped his grandfather's Louisville Slugger and hit a home run with the man's skull. The knife skittered to the floor, and the man collapsed forward.

"Get this fucker off me," Jim said, his voice muffled from the man's belly pressing on his face.

Robbie knelt down and grabbed the man's shoulder with one hand and his hip with the other. The man was heavy. Robbie had to strain, but he finally managed to roll the guy off to the side. Robbie felt the man's neck for a pulse. The guy was out cold, but he was still alive.

"Where's Alison?" Robbie said.

"In there," Jim said, gesturing toward the open door on the other side of the apartment. "She's tied up."

Robbie grabbed the knife from the floor and hurried into the bedroom.

"Oh my god," Alison said. "You guys saved my life."

Robbie started cutting the lengths of rope securing her wrists and ankles. Once Alison was completely free, she sat up and wrapped her arms around Robbie's neck. He returned the hug, and they were still locked in an embrace when a voice from the bedroom doorway said, "Hey, you lovebirds. Forget about me?"

Jim stood there with his hand pressed against his side. He was bleeding. He had been injured during the altercation.

"Oh my god, Jim, are you all right?" Alison said.

"I'm OK. Who was that guy, anyway?"

"Some guy from work. A nurse. His name is Roger Englehart. He came here and attacked me last night."

Apparently Roger Englehart had been stalking Alison. She said she really didn't know much about him, except that his dad was a cop.

"Speaking of which," Robbie said. He reached into his pocket and pulled out his cell phone.

"Wait," Jim said. "Don't call yet."

"Why not? The police need to know about the invasion, and you and the asshole in the living room need an ambulance."

"Just wait. Alison, you say this guy's dad is a cop?"

"That's what I heard. A state trooper."

"Then I think we have a problem."

"He needs medical attention," Robbie said. "And so do you. I'm making the call."

"Wait just a fucking minute," Jim said. "He doesn't need medical attention. He's dead."

"What?"

"I put a couch cushion over his face and smothered his ass."

"Why did you do that?"

"He was starting to stir, and I just—"

"We could have handled him," Robbie said. "There was no need for anyone to die today."

"Yeah, well, someone did die today. A cop's kid, no less. If you call the police, I'll be going to prison. For years. Hell, you know how cops and lawyers are. They're all in cahoots. Roger's father might talk to the DA and get the charge trumped up to murder one, and for that they can go for the death penalty. If you call the police, I'm going to be royally fucked."

"So what are you saying?" Robbie asked.

"I'm saying I have a problem, and I need you guys to help me get rid of it."

"When I walked up here carrying a baseball bat, I thought you were the one I was going to be fighting. I drove up here to St. Augustine because of you."

"So?"

"So now you kill a guy, and you want me to help you?"

"You're not exactly innocent in this whole deal," Jim said. "You bashed the guy in the head with a baseball bat, remember?"

"Yeah, because he was fixing to stab you in the heart."

"This is crazy," Alison said. "Roger was going to kill me. He was going to rape me, and then he was going to kill me. I know he was. He deserved to die, and surely the court will rule what you guys did as self-defense. We just need to call the police and tell them the truth. Right, Robbie?"

Robbie didn't say anything.

"The autopsy's going to show that asphyxiation was the cause of death," Jim said. "I had to press that pillow on his face for several minutes before he finally croaked. I smothered him to death. Nobody's going to call that self-defense."

"So what do you want us to do?" Robbie asked.

"We have to get rid of the body," Jim said. "We have to get him out of here."

"They'll find him," Robbie said. "They always do. No matter where we hide him, they'll find him eventually."

"I have an idea," Jim said. "You guys know that serial killer they call The Zombie?"

"Yeah," Robbie said. "They call him that because all his victims' brains are missing."

"Right," Jim said. "And in every one of those murders, asphyxiation was the primary cause of death."

"So you want to make it look like The Zombie did it?" Alison said.

"Why not? They still haven't caught the guy. It'll look like he did it, and we'll be in the clear."

Robbie and Alison were reluctant, but they finally agreed to help Jim make it appear as though The Zombie had killed Roger Englehart. They agreed, and then they made a pact to take the secret to their graves.

CHAPTER THIRTY-FIVE

Wesley West had been pacing the floor as he told the story. He stopped, folded his arms across his chest, and stared into space.

"They copied me," he said. "They screwed up my entire order of operations. That's why I had to deal with them. Do you understand now?"

"Let me get this straight," I said. "Jim Ballard was trying to get Phineas Carter to tell him where Alison had moved to, and while he was doing that he accidentally shot Phin in the head."

"Correct."

"Then Jim and Alison and Robbie and Roger Englehart all ended up in Alison's apartment in St. Augustine, and Jim and Alison and Robbie conspired to make it look as though *you* killed Roger, who had been stalking Alison and was in the process of assaulting her when Jim arrived."

"Correct."

"So you somehow figured out that Jim and Robbie and Alison were the ones who copycatted you. Once you were sure of that, you moved into Alison's apartment complex to have a nice, convenient home base. Then you went after them one by one. First Alison, and then Jim. Robbie would have been next, but the police got to him first. Now they think *he's* responsible for all the Zombie killings."

"Correct. And it's just not fair. Robbie Asbury is going to get credit for all my hard work. He has inadvertently stolen my moment in the sun. I can't let that go on. Soon, the world will know that I am the real Zombie. The one and only original. I've decided, just now, to make you my final victim, Nicholas. My swan song, so to speak."

"How will the cops know that *you're* not the copycat?" I said.

"Because I'll confess to all the murders except Roger Englehart's. They'll be able to verify that I was in all those locations."

Because Freak Willy was in all those locations, I thought.

They say truth is stranger than fiction, and Wesley West's story was certainly more bizarre than any novel I'd ever read or any movie I'd ever seen. It had a little bit of everything, including cannibalism.

"If you're going to turn yourself in anyway, why don't you just let me go?" I said. "What's the point of a swan song? I thought we were friends."

He didn't respond. He kept staring into space. He seemed to be in some sort of trance now. He seemed to be in his own little depraved universe.

Without saying another word, he put his shoes on and walked out of the bedroom, pulling the door shut on his way out. I heard the front door open and close. I assumed he was going down to his car, to look for the saw he'd mentioned. The saw he would use to remove the top of my skull.

I knew I didn't have much time. If the tool was in the car, it would only take him a few minutes to retrieve it and come back to the apartment. Then he would go to work on me.

I stared at the bottle of acetone Wesley had left on the floor by the dresser. It was only a couple of feet away from me, but it might as well have been a mile. My hands and feet were hopelessly stuck to the floor.

The only way for me to move, the only possible way out of this predicament, was to do myself bodily harm. They say a coyote will chew its own leg off to free itself from a steel trap. In essence, that's what I was going to have to do.

I looked down at my right foot. It was the one closest to the dresser. Closest to the bottle of acetone. I tried to lift it gently, a little at a time, and right away I felt the delicate skin near my little toe start to tear. I clenched my teeth and growled. Not really a growl, more of a sustained guttural moan from deep in my chest. The pain was unbearable. I didn't think I could do it. Not even to save my life.

I wondered if it would be better to just rip my foot from the floor in a single rapid motion, the way you tear off a Band-Aid. The pain would be severe for a second, but then it would quickly subside. That was the theory. I decided to go for it. I closed my eyes, tensed every muscle in my body, and yanked my foot away from the floor with a quick jerk.

A bright light exploded behind my eyeballs as a red-hot bolus of molten pain seared through every nerve in my body. I thought I was going to hurl for sure this time, but I managed to swallow it back. I looked down at my foot. There was skin and tissue missing from the side, and it was bleeding profusely. The pain was intense, and it got more and more severe as the seconds ticked by. The Band-Aid theory hadn't panned out. The reverse was happening. The pain was getting worse.

I looked at the floor. There was a thin strip of bloody flesh where my foot had been. Seconds earlier it had been part of me, but now it appeared foreign. Like a cut of raw meat in a butcher's case.

My peripheral vision narrowed. I thought I was going to pass out. There was no way I could rip my other foot away from the floor, or my hands. It wasn't going to happen. I would lose consciousness from the pain, and Wesley West would make sure I never woke up.

My eyes stung from the sweat dripping into them, and my foot felt as though someone had taken a cheese grater to it. I took a couple of deep breaths, trying to muster the strength to carry on.

I stretched my leg to the right and tried to hook my foot around the can of acetone. With every heartbeat, a trillion needles pierced the side of my sole. With every second that passed, my mind came closer to shutting down. I stretched and stretched until the skin on my other foot was on the verge of tearing, but it was no use. The acetone was a couple of inches beyond my reach.

I heard the click of the deadbolt, and I knew this was it. The Zombie was back, and I was going to die.

CHAPTER THIRTY-SIX

Marshal Mack Chillin walks through the swinging saloon doors. Everyone in the town has abandoned him. He alone must face the ruthless gang of thugs now. They're all sitting at the bar, drinking beer and whiskey and having a hooting good time. There's laughter and backslapping and a guy wearing a white shirt and suspenders playing an upbeat tune on the piano.

A hush falls over the room as Mack steps forward.

"I told you boys to move along," Mack says. "I'm going to give you one more chance to leave peacefully."

"And I told you we were going to have a beer first," says Rex. He stands and faces Mack.

We see a close-up of Mack's right hand, his fingers rock steady and only inches from the stag grips on his nickel-plated revolver.

We see a close-up of Rex's hand, his fingers twitching and only inches from the rosewood grips on his black steel revolver...

Wesley West didn't come back to the bedroom right away. He was talking to someone on the phone.

"Can't do it tonight. There's no way. I'm busy with something else."

I decided to make one last push. I stretched for all I was worth, and the tip of my big toe touched the lip of the metal acetone can. The pain shooting through me was like nothing I'd ever felt. I imagined it was similar to being eaten alive by fire ants. It was impossible to ignore, but I blocked it best I could and focused on pressing my toe against the can.

Stretching, straining, sweating, hurting, I finally got the right amount of leverage. The can tilted, and then toppled sideways. Now I could reach it with my foot.

"I'm telling you, Felix. I can't do it. You'll have to find someone else."

Felix was the manager at the hotel lounge. He must have been trying to get Wesley to come in and play. Josie and the Pussycats must have canceled.

Through the feverish haze of the worst pain of my life, I kicked the acetone can with my heel. It slid freely on the hardwood floor, spinning and coming to a stop inches from my face. I leaned toward it and used my tongue to position it, and then I bit down hard on the plastic pouring spout. I hoped it wouldn't open and spill out into my mouth. That would have been the most ironic thing ever. I would have died from ingesting the solvent. I would have died trying to save myself. But I got lucky. The spout didn't open and the acetone didn't trickle down my throat and kill me. I lifted the can, my jaw and neck muscles burning against the strain, and nestled it into my right armpit.

"You can't fire me for not coming in on one of my nights off. I have a contract. I'll sue your ass."

I was breathing hard, and my foot felt as though someone had jammed a box of razor blades into it. I leaned over and bit down on the little plastic tab that was supposed to pop the little plastic lid off the little plastic pouring spout. I bit down on it with all my might. I pulled and tugged and jerked until I thought my front teeth were going to break off at the gumlines. Finally, the lid popped open, and the beautiful noxious fumes of acetone filled the air.

I used my neck and shoulder muscles to tilt the spout away from my face, and seconds later I felt the cold liquid spilling along my right side. It oozed around my hand, and I felt the skin on my palm start to loosen from its adherence to the floor. I rocked my hand back and forth and made a massaging motion with it and enough of the acetone seeped in and suddenly my right hand was free. I quickly snatched the can and doused the areas around my left hand and left foot.

Now I was free to move around.

I got busy.

A couple of minutes went by before I heard Wesley's voice again. "Then there's nothing left for us to talk about," he said. "The next call you'll be getting will be from my attorney. Good-bye."

Silence.

I watched as the doorknob slowly turned counterclockwise, listened as the bolting mechanism slid out of the latch hole and whispered past the strike plate.

The door creaked open, and The Zombie walked in.

The tool he held looked something like a dentist's drill, but there was a serrated blade about the size of a quarter near its motorized tip. A power cord dangled from the other end, and the whole apparatus was dotted with what appeared to be dried blood.

The first thing Wesley noticed was the smell. The entire can of acetone was on the floor, and the air was thick with its toxic fumes. He made a groaning sound as he hooded his nose with his free hand.

His eyes darted left and right. "What the—"

Before he could say *fuck*, I hobbled forward on one leg and smashed him in the face with the butt of Jim Ballard's revolver. I'd checked, and there weren't any bullets in the gun, but it made a fine blunt instrument. It was dirty and rusty and I would have been afraid to fire it anyway. It might have blown up in my hand.

Wesley's surgical saw went skittering across the floor, and Wesley fell to his knees. I'd clouted him pretty hard, but somehow he remained conscious.

"I should crack your skull like an egg and feed your *own* brain to you," I said. "Talk about a fucking swan song."

His eyes were crossed. Blood and drool dribbled from the corner of his mouth. "Do it," he said. "Go ahead, kill me. Look at me. I'm helpless, so go ahead and finish the job."

He paused. He dropped to the floor confusedly and sat cross-legged.

"But you won't," he said. "You don't have it in you. You're too much of a pussy."

I limped backward, nearly losing my balance, and sat on the edge of the bed. The adrenaline surge had momentarily taken the edge off the pain in my foot.

"You know what the difference is between you and me?" I said. "Besides the fact that I'm a great guitar player and you suck donkey dicks? The difference between you and me is that you're a murderer and I'm not. I've killed men before, Wesley, but never in cold blood. I'm the guy in the white hat. I'm the good guy. And motherfucker, the good guy always wins."

But even as the words left my mouth, I knew it wasn't true.

We see a close-up of Mack's right hand, his fingers rock steady and only inches from the stag grips on his nickel-plated revolver.

We see a close-up of Rex's hand, his fingers twitching and only inches from the rosewood grips on his black steel revolver.

Rex makes the first move, but Mack beats him to the draw. Mack fires three times in quick succession, and each bullet hits Rex like a sledgehammer. He staggers sideways, sweeps the top of the bar with his arm, and sends glasses and bottles crashing to the floor. He twists and flails and gyrates and coughs up bloody chunks of his last meal, and finally he crumples. He collapses on his back and stares at the ceiling with lifeless eyes. Rex is dead. Again.

A whiff of smoke rises from the barrel of Mack's gun. He blows on it, holsters the piece, and turns toward the other zombies.

"There's no need for any more bloodshed. Now get the fuck out of my town."

The zombies put their hats on. They saunter away, single file, through the swinging saloon doors. Off to wreak havoc in another time period.

There's a sense of relief as the concluding music starts to play, and as the final credits start to roll. Mack Chillin has saved the day. The town is safe now. Mack is a hero, and everything can go back to normal.

If Joe Crawford's dad had started the car then, if we had left the drive-in theater at that moment—as everyone except the teenagers making out in the back row did—then that's what we would have thought. That the town was safe. That Mack was a hero.

But Joe's dad happened to be a film buff. He liked to know who the key grip was, and who designed the costumes. He liked to know who did the sound and the makeup and the editing. All that crap. So we sat there and waited, our bellies full of generic soda pop and cheese puffs, and our sleepy young minds full of gratuitous blood and gore.

At least the good guy had won. That's what we thought.

But that's not what happened. The credits were rolling, but the movie wasn't over.

Mack leaves the saloon, and walks back toward his office. Some of the townspeople come out from hiding and gradually start filling the dusty street. Everyone's smiling, and some of the men and women walk up to Mack and pat him on the back. They congratulate him for a job well done. Now they can return to their mundane and laborious nineteenth-century lives. It's back to business as usual in Dodge City, Kansas.

But wait.

The zombie known as Boomer swoops by on his horse and decapitates a pretty young woman with a Bowie knife. Her head tumbles from her shoulders and rolls away, leaving a bright red trail of blood in the dust.

Mack goes for his gun, but the zombie named Grady lassos him and drags him to the ground. We see Mack lying in the street, struggling to get loose as the band of semi-dead cannibals descends on him.

As the screen fades to black, we hear chomping and slurping and a final, "Yee haw!"

The End.

In hindsight, Mack Chillin should have shot every one of those brain-sucking sons of bitches while they were still inside the Short Twig Saloon. Mack had already unloaded three rounds on Rex. So, he should have picked three more of them off, reloaded, and kept firing until the whole bloodthirsty pack was exterminated. Mack should have killed them all when he had a chance. None of them was armed, except Rex, so Mack could have gone down the row and dropped every one of them like ducks in a shooting gallery. He should have sentenced them to death on the spot. It wasn't like there was any hope for rehabilitation. Not with those motherfuckers.

And not with Wesley West.

Wesley had smothered thirteen people to death. He had sawed the tops of their skulls off and scooped their brains out. He had reattached the tops of said skulls with the same adhesive he'd used to glue me to the floor, and then he had eaten their brains. No amount of psychological counseling or vocational training was going to cure that.

I decided it was time to take off my white hat.

I grabbed the Fender Telecaster from its stand and used it for a cane. I shuffled over to the dresser, yanked open the drawer second from the bottom, reached in, and pulled out what I wanted.

Wesley was babbling on incoherently about something. I tried to ignore him. I hobbled to the bedroom doorway, pulled the pin, and tossed the Vietnam-era fragment grenade onto his lap.

I slammed the door shut and limped frantically for the exit.

CHAPTER THIRTY-SEVEN

Fortunately for me, hand grenades don't really blow whole buildings up like they do in the movies. There was a loud boom, followed by the sound of shrapnel hitting Sheetrock. And that was it. I waited in my car for a few minutes, but there was no indication that the blast had even started a fire. I figured Wesley's body had absorbed most of it. The police would find the Krazy Glue and the acetone and the saw and the human brain pâté, and the Zombie mystery would be solved.

For real this time.

The next morning, I dropped the Ford Focus off at the rental car office and took a cab to the police station. I showed up at Detective Craig P. Sullivan's office promptly at eight o'clock.

"What happened to you?" Sullivan said.

"I stepped on a shell at the beach."

From Wesley's apartment I'd driven to Walgreens and purchased a pair of crutches and a surgical boot and the necessary supplies to dress my foot. I'd taken some Advil, but it still hurt like hell.

"Have a seat, Colt."

Sullivan was at his desk. I sat in the padded seat across from him.

"How long do you think this is going to take?" I said.

"Not long. Actually, there's been a major new development. Just overnight."

"Really? What's that?"

"I can't talk about it. Let's just say Robbie Asbury might not be The Zombie after all. We still want to cover all the bases, though. We still need a formal statement from you."

"I thought you were sure it was Robbie. A hundred percent."

"I might have been wrong. It happens. Not very often, but it happens."

"Did Robbie tell you what he was doing in Fort Lauderdale?" I said.

"No. He's all lawyered up now. He's not telling us much of anything."

I handed Sullivan a slip of paper. "He was at this address, looking at a classic BMW that formerly belonged to Jim Ballard. You might want to check it out."

"All right. I will."

I had a hunch the car had been used to transport Roger Englehart's body from St. Augustine to Brunswick. The blood flakes in my little screwdriver case might have been enough to confirm it, but I had collected them illegally. Robbie's lawyer would have a field day if something like that was ever presented as evidence in court. Better to let the police check the car out and gather the evidence the right way. There was plenty more dried blood where mine had come from.

"So there's a new suspect in the Zombie case?" I said.

"Listen to the news later. You'll find out along with everyone else. Was there something else you wanted to tell me? You said there were a couple of things."

I handed him another slip of paper. Written on it was the tag number of the SUV that had delivered Veronica to Dan the Van Man.

"I stumbled upon some kind of pornography ring," I said. "They're using runaways. Promising them stardom and all that shit. I imagine some of them are underage. I have some digital photographs too, taken at the drop point on A1A. Just give me your e-mail address and—"

"You stumbled upon it, huh?"

"Yeah."

"Look, Colt, I've been on to you for a while now. It didn't take a lot of research. I know you were a famous guitar player once upon a time, and I know you were a private investigator. I know you lost your license over a narcotics conviction. I could lock you up right now if I wanted to. So cut the bullshit, all right?"

"If you knew, why did you let me—"

"I thought you were dead, remember? Let's start all over. Why did you come to Key West?"

"I was hired to investigate the murder of a man named Phineas Carter," I said.

I told him everything, up to the point where I left the hotel last night and drove to Wesley West's apartment. I left all that out. I figured he would arrest me for sure if he knew I'd blown Wesley up with a hand grenade. But I spilled my guts about everything else. Everything except the sexual assault. I fudged on the facts about that night. I told him I was watching Daniel Chard's house when I heard shouting and gunshots, followed by utter silence.

"I waited for a few minutes, and then walked over and peeked into a window," I said. "It was total carnage in there. Blood everywhere. I thought maybe the girl was still alive, so I walked inside to make sure. But it was too late. She was dead. I found a pay phone after that and made an anonymous call to the police."

"And you think someone in this pornography ring was responsible for killing Phineas Carter?" he said.

"Right."

I didn't think that anymore, of course, but I couldn't tell Sullivan what I knew. I couldn't tell him that Jim Ballard was the one who had blown Phin's brains out. I couldn't tell him without revealing what had happened last night. I figured the cops would put it all together soon enough, once they sifted through the evidence in Wesley's apartment. I figured they would be able to trace the rusty revolver back to Jim. It must have been registered. He wouldn't have bothered burying it otherwise. I figured the cops would put it all together, and there really wasn't any hurry. Jim Ballard wasn't going anywhere. He was a brainless corpse in the morgue now.

In the meantime, the cops could round up the scumbags making porn flicks with runaways.

"I'll get Vice to follow up on that SUV," Sullivan said. "I appreciate the tip."

He wrote his e-mail address on a Post-it and handed it to me.

I looked at my watch. "I'd really like to hit the road soon," I said. "Can we get this over with?"

"Sure. Let's walk over to the interview room."

We walked over to the interview room, and Sullivan taped my statement regarding the day Alison Palmer was found dead in her apartment. After that, Sullivan talked to someone at the impound lot and convinced them to release the hold on my GMC Jimmy. I drove back to the hotel and loaded all my things and then stopped at the front desk to check out. The sign beside the hallway leading to the lounge still said *Wesley West, Sunday and Monday night.* I guessed they hadn't gotten the memo.

I grabbed a cup of coffee and a bagel from the free continental breakfast, climbed into my car, and began the long journey home.

CHAPTER THIRTY-EIGHT

I tried to call Wanda Taylor from the highway, but she didn't answer her phone. I left a message, and an hour later Lonnie called me back.

"She's not doing very well," he said. "I had to take her to the hospital last night."

"You're still up in New York?" I said.

"Yeah. She's been kind of in and out all day. Sometimes she's with it, other times she doesn't even recognize me."

"Next time she's with it, tell her a man named Jim Ballard killed her father."

"Let me write this down," Lonnie said. "Jim Fowler?"

"*Ballard*," I said. I spelled it out for him. "He had been looking for his ex-girlfriend, who had subleased her apartment to Wanda's biological father."

"Phineas Carter."

"Right. Jim Ballard and Phineas Carter didn't even know each other. Phin just happened to get in the way during one of Ballard's jealous fits of rage. Supposedly the shooting was an accident, but we'll never know for sure."

"Why's that?"

"Because Jim Ballard is dead now too."

"I thought that name sounded familiar. He was one of The Zombie's victims, right? One of the recent ones."

"Yeah. Listen, Lonnie, this is all confidential, OK? I don't want you to tell anyone what I've told you. Except Wanda, of course."

"Sure, man. I understand."

"Tell her justice was served, in a way. I can't condone The Zombie's actions, of course, but Jim Ballard pretty much got what was coming to him."

We talked music for a few minutes, trying to take the edge off the woeful situation. I told him to give me a call if there was any change in Wanda's condition. He knew what I meant.

* * *

Sunday morning I woke up next to the most beautiful woman in the world. I snuggled in close behind her.

"Is that a baseball bat, or you just glad to see me?" she said.

"You know what I want."

"And I know what you're not going to get. Not for the next few days, anyway."

"Just this once?"

"No, Nicholas. That's gross. We already had this discussion last night. Now leave me alone."

"I guess I'll have to take matters into my own hands," I said.

"You do that. I'm going back to sleep."

She was being extremely difficult.

"I thought you would be more excited to have me home," I said.

She turned around and kissed me. "I am excited to have you home. But you know how I feel about that. Anyway, I have a surprise for you. Actually, I have two surprises."

"For me?"

"Yes."

"Big surprises or little surprises?"

"Huge surprises," she said.

Juliet fell back to sleep, and a few minutes later I got up and took a shower and started a pot of coffee. I was getting around OK without the crutches, but I was still wearing the surgical boot. I was on my third cup of coffee when she finally came dragging into the kitchen.

"Good morning," I said.

"Morning. You want me to fix you some breakfast?"

"I want my surprises."

She laughed. "You're such a little boy sometimes," she said. "All right, I'll get ready and then we'll go."

"We have to go somewhere?"

"You'll see."

Juliet took a shower and got dressed. We took her car, and she drove. As we made our way along State Road 21, something occurred to me, and I couldn't believe I hadn't thought of it sooner. I'd had unprotected sex with a woman I knew absolutely nothing about. I wondered how many other men Veronica had been with in the previous weeks. Months. Years. There was no telling. The humiliation of being forced to have intercourse on camera must have traumatized that little issue right out of my mind.

Thinking about it made me furious. I was angry that I had been put in a position where I had to worry about such a thing, and I was angry at myself for not thinking more clearly. If Juliet hadn't been on her period, I would have put her at risk as well.

She steered into a strip mall, and parked in front of H&R Block.

"We're having tax troubles?" I said. "That's my surprise?"

"No, silly. Look."

She pointed at the *FOR LEASE* sign in the window.

"Oh," I said.

"Come on."

We climbed out of the car. It was a nice November afternoon, sunny and crisp and seventy-some degrees, a picture-perfect example of what passes for fall in this part of the country. Juliet pulled a set of keys out of her purse and opened the door, and we walked into the long and narrow space that was once a tax preparer's office.

"What do you think?" she said.

"It's a vacant store. What am I supposed to think?"

"We'll fix it up. This can be your teaching studio."

"Teaching studio?"

"For guitar lessons," she said. "Like we talked about on the phone."

I couldn't believe it. Juliet knew how miserable I'd been the past few months, with nothing much to do. She knew I needed something meaningful to fill my days, something that would give me a sense of purpose. Something that would make me feel like a man again. I'd told myself I would never teach, but suddenly it didn't seem like such a bad idea. Maybe all I had needed was a nudge in the right direction from the right person. What the hell, I thought. I would give it a try. At least for six months.

I felt myself starting to get choked up. "You rented this for me?" I said.

"Yes! We have a six-month lease. Isn't it great?"

"It's wonderful, darling. I swear, I don't deserve you."

We looked around for a while and started discussing what colors to paint the walls, and what would go here and what would go there.

"Are you ready for your other surprise?" Juliet said.

"This is too much already. I can't believe there's more."

"Well, the second surprise is really as much for me as it is for you."

"What is it?" I said.

"Are you ready? I bought a VIP package to see John Fogerty in concert next July. This time, you will get to meet Mr. Fogerty for sure."

I looked into her eyes. "You are something else," I said. "Next July, huh? Where's the concert?"

"That's the best part. It's in Finland!"

"We're going to Europe?"

"Yes, yes, yes. It will be the vacation you promised me."

We stood there for five minutes or so, hugging and kissing like schoolkids between classes.

"Are you happy?" Juliet said.

"Yes, darling. I'm very happy."

I was very happy, but still very concerned. Later that evening, Juliet sensed my melancholy mood, and I shrugged it off as always being like that right after a tough job. She decided food might cheer me up, so she started working on a Filipino noodle dish called *pancit*. My favorite. While she was busy with that, I stepped out on the front porch and called Detective Sullivan.

"What's up?" he said.

"I need a big favor. Like I told you before, I walked into Daniel Chard's house after the shooting and stabbing. I got to thinking about it. I don't think I touched anything, but there was blood everywhere. You know what I'm saying?"

"I think so. You want to know if either of them was HIV positive? Or if they had hepatitis or anything?"

"Exactly. I'm sure they're both coroner's cases, right?"

"Yeah, but it'll be a few days before we get the pathology reports. Maybe even a week."

"Would you give me a call as soon as you know?" I said.

"I'm really not supposed to do that, Colt."

"But you will?"

There was a long pause.

"All right," he said. "But if it ever gets out, I'll hang you by your balls."

He hung up without saying good-bye.

CHAPTER THIRTY-NINE

It was just the three of us for Thanksgiving, but Juliet and Brittney had been busy all morning and afternoon preparing a feast that could have fed an army. I was sitting at the computer in the living room, looking at some examples of teaching manuals for guitar. I planned to eventually write my own series of books, but for now I would need something to get started with.

I'd tacked some flyers on the bulletin board at one of local music stores, and I'd gotten over twenty calls in just a couple of days. Apparently a lot of people were interested in taking lessons from a bona fide rock star, even an aging and somewhat crippled one. I charged a little more than most of the guys around town, but I figured I was worth it. At fifty dollars for half an hour, I already had enough students to make the rent.

"Dad, are you OK?"

It was Brittney. She had somehow walked in from the kitchen without me noticing. I wondered how long she had been standing behind me.

"I'm all right," I said. "Just checking out some of these guitar books."

Brittney's long blond hair was tied back in a single braid. She'd fixed it for working in the kitchen all day.

She sighed. "You've just been acting weird since I got home yesterday. Did I do something to make you mad?"

I stood and gave her a hug. "Of course not, sweetheart. I've just had a lot on my mind lately. I guess I'm not in much of a holiday mood. Sorry."

"Did I tell you Carl Hiaasen was on campus a couple of weeks ago?"

"Yeah, I was talking to you on the phone when you were waiting for him to come on. Remember?"

"Oh, that's right. But I don't think I ever told you how funny he was. He was freaking hilarious. I thought I was going to pee my pants."

She told me some of the things the famous writer had said. I smiled and chuckled when I was supposed to, but I think she could tell my heart really wasn't in it.

"I'm going to have to read something by him one of these days," I said. "If I can ever find the time."

"I think it's good you're going to be busy now."

"I think so too."

"I heard you playing awhile ago. It sounded great."

"Thanks," I said.

She was trying to cheer me up, but I knew better. What I'd been playing earlier didn't sound great. Not to a trained ear, anyway. The scales I'd been refamiliarizing myself with sounded like they were being played by a guy with eight screws holding his fingers together.

"Daddy, want to hear a joke I made up?"

"Sure," I said.

"A sandwich staggers into a bar. The bartender looks up and says, 'Let me call you a cab, buddy. You're toasted.'"

I kept waiting for more. I was so preoccupied, I didn't even get it.

Juliet shouted from the kitchen. "OK, you two. Time to eat."

Brittney and I walked to the dining room. Juliet was placing silverware on cloth napkins by the plates. The napkins were white, not burgundy, but they still reminded me of the ones at Wesley West's house.

"Can I help you with anything?" I said.

"You can carry the turkey in."

I carried the turkey in. It was a big bird on a big platter. I set it on the table. There was cranberry sauce and oyster stuffing and green-bean casserole and a dish of candied yams. Mashed potatoes, gravy, stuffed mushrooms. Three pies and a jug of chardonnay. Everything looked great and smelled great, but all I could think about was human brain pâté smeared on crackers, and that I might have contracted a deadly disease from Veronica. She was a beautiful girl, and it broke my heart that she had gotten mixed up with Dan and his seedy crowd. I was saddened by the fact that she had died violently and needlessly at such a young age, but I couldn't help worrying that she might have given me something that would turn my life—and Juliet's—upside down.

The table was lovely and the food was lovely, but I didn't have much of an appetite. I hadn't had much of one since I'd been home.

"Carve us some turkey, and I'll pour the wine," Juliet said.

"You guys want white meat or dark meat?" I said.

The both wanted white. I sliced off some breast meat for them and put it on their plates, and then I cut off a drumstick for myself. I chose some cranberry sauce and oyster stuffing to go with it.

We all sat down. I took a sip of wine.

"Would you like to say the blessing?" Juliet said.

"Let's just eat," I said.

My downbeat attitude finally set her off. Apparently she'd grown tired of trying to walk on eggshells while I wallowed in despondence.

"What the hell is wrong with you?" she said.

"Let's just fucking eat."

She tensed, gave me a hard stare.

"I'll say the blessing," Brittney said, ever the peacemaker. "Dad's being a poophead for some reason."

My cell phone vibrated in my pocket. I pulled it out and looked at it, got up, and started walking toward the front door.

"I better take this," I said.

"Can't you just turn it off while we're having dinner?" Juliet said. "It's Thanksgiving, Nicholas."

"It's probably another customer. I'll be back in a minute."

I knew it wasn't another customer. It was a Key West area code. Key Death, I thought. Those smart-ass radio guys were still calling it that. I stepped out on the porch.

"Hello?" I said.

"Hey, Colt. Craig Sullivan. Sorry to call you on the holiday. I got those patho results a couple of days ago, and I've been so busy—"

"Just tell me," I said.

He told me.

The news was not good.

CHAPTER FORTY

The news was not good.

The news was *great.*

I breathed a sigh of relief and went back and took my place at the head of the dinner table.

And this time, I had a smile on my face.

I said the blessing, and Brittney giggled when I thanked God for dolphins. Brittney giggled, and then we all started laughing. We couldn't help it.

It was, without a doubt, the best Thanksgiving ever.

THE END

ACKNOWLEDGMENTS

There's no better feeling than to see months of painstaking work come to fruition in the form of a published book. And, as always, it could only have happened with a little help from my friends.

Thanks to Jane Dystel and Miriam Goderich for their ongoing support. A good literary agent is crucial in building an author's career, and these are two of the best.

Thanks to Andy Bartlett, Jacque Ben-Zekry, Charlotte Herscher, and all the other wonderful folks at Thomas & Mercer. Your tireless efforts make my work shine.

Thanks to all my friends, family members, and peers, for their continuing support. Please forgive me if I've forgotten anyone. Corey Hardin, Kathy Ledford, Sue Mudd, Stephen Parrish, Erica Orloff, Joe Konrath, Mark Terry, Jon VanZile, Dan Peters, Kathy Blue Quindoza, David Ryan, Scott Nicholson, David Morrell, Lee Goldberg, Bill Rabkin, Melody Woods Raymond, Nita Bingham, Norm Kelly, Mike Priddy, Alan Orloff, Jane Driskell, Allison Brennan, Blake Crouch, Bud Elder, Char Chaffin, Dana King, Denise Puthuff, Eric Christopherson, Dusty Rhoades, LaDonna

Koebel, Lainey Bancroft, Linda McCandless, Tess Gerritsen, Tammy Downard, Trish Barr Johns, Pete Helow…and so many more. At one time or another, every one of you has touched my life in amazing ways, and the ongoing journey would not be the same without you.

ABOUT THE AUTHOR

Pete Helow, 2011

Jude Hardin is coauthor of the Dead Man series of adventure/horror thrillers created by Lee Goldberg and William Rabkin. His debut novel featuring Nicholas Colt—*Pocket-47*—received a starred review from *Publishers Weekly*. *The New York Times* best-selling author Tess Gerritsen wrote, "*Pocket-47* sucked me in and held me enthralled...[Nicholas Colt] is a character I'm eager to follow." And David Morrell, creator of *Rambo*, called the second Nicholas Colt thriller, *Crosscut*, "fast, fierce, and relentless." Hardin has held down a variety of jobs—from drummer to chemical plant supervisor to freelance journalist—each of which fuels his writing. When he isn't creating his next story, he enjoys fishing with his son. He lives in north Florida.